A Federal Agent Mystery

THE SPY & COUNTERSPY FILE

Clarence Budington Kelland

Digital Parchment Press

THE FEDERAL AGENT MYSTERIES

IN THE 1950s Kelland was asked to write a series giving people a behind-the-scenes look at what different types of federal law enforcement agents—the FBI, Postal Service, Park rangers, Secret Service, etc.—did to earn their keep. During the writing, he was allowed unprecedented access to offices, procedures, agents and files—and so the stories in this series are not only fascinating and compelling, but richly detailed, filled with "fine documentary stuff" *(The Criminal Record).*

The Counterfeit Gentleman File
(The Secret Service)

The Sinister Strangers File
(The National Park Service)

The Spy and Counterspy File
(The CIA, White Sands Missile Testing Range)

The Great Mail Robbery File
(The U.S. Post Office)

The Murdered G-Man File
(The FBI— Acclaimed *Saturday Evening Post* serial)

A Digital Parchment Services publication
ISBN 9781545446034
Copyright 1953, renewed 1981
First serialized in *The Saturday Evening Post* 1955, issued in hardcover by Dodd, Mead & Co. 1961.

All rights reserved. This book may not be reproduced in whole or in part without written permission. Published under license of the estate of Clarence Budington Kelland.

Note: Because English is a living language, it experiences continual change and evolution. Spelling, punctuation and construction have changed in many respects in the 60 years since this novel was written. We have made every effort to preserve the author's original text in order to give an accurate sense of its context and era.

Published as *Spy and Counterspy* in magazine and in hardcover.

Publisher's Dedication—

To

Michael Judd,

loyal keeper of the flame

USAG2 File #Y53-8782

Year: 1953

Locale: White Sands NM U.S. Rocket Testing Grounds

Agent: Thomas A. E. Gimp, U.S. Army G-2
(temporarily assigned)

Case status: CLOSED

Part One

I AM not given to making sociological observations, because my field is electronics—specifically as it applies to high-altitude navigation. But I am compelled to remark that a brat can exert a profound influence upon the occupants of the club car of a railroad train. This particular brat was about six years old and his youthful mother regarded his antics with pride.

He first attracted my attention by rushing to the front of the car, turning suddenly and shouting in a menacing voice, "Stick 'em up! This is a holdup!" When he noted the surprised expressions upon our faces, he exulted, "Scared the daylights out of you, didn't I?"

I had just settled myself to the reading of a restricted pamphlet written by Doctor Lucius Boomister, of the Rocket Sonde Branch of Naval Research, entitled *The Atmospheric Ocean,* but, much to my annoyance, found myself totally unable to concentrate. I had saved this pamphlet, with certain others, as lighter reading to while away the tedium of travel. I hoped that the mother of the little monster would exert a restraining influence upon him, possibly by applying her palm to a suitable area of his person, but she did not do so.

The brat altered his character, ceasing to be a criminal and becoming a pest. He walked down the car, which was but sparsely occupied, stopping before each passenger and demanding, "Play cards with me? I bet I can beat the stuffing out of you."

"He is so friendly," his mother said audibly.

I cleared my throat. "I would apply quite a different epithet to his manners."

This seemed to bring no beneficial result. Upon being rebuffed by all, the young person converted himself into what I took to be a dive bomber and rushed the length of the car uttering discordant sounds. The car gave a lurch and the bomber crashed, not, to my disappointment, colliding with something very hard which might have produced unconsciousness, but butting my neighbor in the midsection.

My neighbor chanced to be a young woman whom I had not heretofore noted. She uttered a distressed noise which sounded like the syllable "Oaf." I noted that she was tangled in a complicated manner with the brat. Quite naturally I relieved her of the incubus, and then, yielding to impulse, laid him across my knee and cuffed his posterior enjoyably. The enjoyment was not his. He emitted horrible shrieks, and, upon being released, kicked me upon the shin and called me a name which I shall not repeat.

"I wish," said a gentleman across the aisle, "that I had done that mayhem."

"It probably," I replied, "will involve me in a suit for damages for assault and battery."

"I," said the young woman adjoining me, "will cheerfully be witness for the defense."

I do not commonly engage in conversation with utter strangers, not from any tendency toward misanthropy, but because I have found that very few of them have anything to say of interest, and that, generally, they display an abysmal ignorance of what I myself have to offer in a conversational way. However, I found myself involved. I seemed to have brought upon myself a species of popularity.

There comes in the life of every human being, or so I imagine, a critical instant—a moment causing a more or less important alteration in himself, in his attitude toward life, and a definite alteration in the trend of his future. I may say, without fear of successful contradiction, that such a modifying moment in my own career arrived with the impact of my palm against the brat's bottom. For it caused the intrusion into my orbit of the man Balthasar Toledo, who was not so much a human being as the romanticized picture of a human being; and of the exotic and bewildering Renee du Guesclin. Until that second I had been much more concerned with the troposphere and the stratosphere and the ionosphere than I was with individuals or with events occurring upon the surface of earth.

Melinna says, quite absurdly, that I am the hero of the events which befell at White Sands, of which, so far as I was concerned, the cuffing of a boy's bottom on the Golden State Limited was the commencement. I became involved inadvertently and unwillingly. A knowledge of my character and antecedents will convince that no one could be more adverse than I to adventure, violence or romance.

Therefore it seems in order to refute the charges that I have been impetuous, meddlesome, rash and belligerent, and at the very beginning to set forth the sort of individual I am, how my character was formed both by heredity and by environment; and how qualities of mildness, studiousness and even timidity have been greviously misrepresented by irresponsible persons as their very contraries.

The young woman at my left who was butted in the stomach by the brat was Renee du Gueselin; the gentleman opposite me was none other than Balthasar Toledo. I have been informed that their presence was not mere blind chance, but the result of intention. It may be so. However that may be, let me produce my own defense.

There was, I am informed, considerable debate prior to my christening. My four uncles, my two aunts and my father are eminent in their several fields and each proposed a name for myself. My uncles Spencer and Spinoza are eminent in the field of philosophy; my uncles Archimedes and Aristotle are professors of pure science and are engaged in atomic research; my Aunt Zenobia, a historian, is president of a considerable college for young women, and my Aunt Aspasia is not without fame in the field of paleontology. My father, who deserted the academic field to become research chemist for a great corporation, proposed that I should be named Nikola Tesla. Others of my relatives put forward such appellations as Solon, Mercator, Bacon, Volta as fitting names for a baby with an ancestry such as mine.

But my mother, a tiny woman with a big determination, put down her foot. "If," she said, "my baby must be burdened with a name eminent in science, philosophy or invention, as seems to be the determination of this self-elected Sanhedrin, then it shall be a name he can write in a hotel register without wincing."

"Nonsense, my precious," expostulated my father.

"His name," said my mother with firmness that bordered upon the adamantine, "shall be Thomas Alva Edison. Then, at least, his boy friends can call him Tom. It may be my son is predestined for an academic life, but at least I shall start him out with a name that gives him a faint chance to become a normal human being and not a piece of animated laboratory equipment."

I am told by an eyewitness that at this point my mother drew me to her and held me close and gazed at her relatives-in-law with some hostility. "Tommy," she said to me, "I hope that your horizon will not be the walls of a laboratory or a study. I pray that you will experience some of the lovely blunders that give zest to life. I trust that you will learn by experience that a kiss may be as potent as a cosmic ray; and that before you come to an age of full discretion, you will walk among the emotions of love and fear and hatred and awe and ambition and reverence. And not"—and here I imagine her fine gray eyes flashed defiantly—"become a desiccated container for dangerous theories which had best not be meddled with. Now, all of you, clear out. I am about to perform that remarkable chemical experiment of administering nourishment to my offspring."

So it came about that I bear the name of Thomas Alva Edison Gimp, but my mother, determined as she is, has been potent to modify only in the slightest degree my destiny to become a wanderer in the limitless wilderness of science.

Had it not been for my mother's insistence, I would not have been equipped to cope with certain desperate matters that occurred in the fastnesses of the Organ Mountains. But she could do nothing to prepare me for the complexities that arose incident to the startling reappearance of Melinna in my orbit.

"They," my mother said, referring to my uncles and aunts,

"do not realize that the mind is contained in a body, and that an efficient body can be very valuable to an individual, as well as provide him with numerous desirable pleasures."

She was able to compel me, in my spare time, to indulge in certain physical exercises, and even to induce me to take part in various athletic endeavors in my college; with the result, so she claims, that I am the largest and bulkiest of all the Gimp family. My height upon becoming of age was six feet and one inch, and my weight was a hundred and ninety-eight pounds. But in her secondary purpose, which was to inculcate in me an appreciation and understanding of romance, she failed utterly. And this in spite of the fact that I studied obediently and attentively such treatises upon the subject as *Ivanhoe, Treasure Island, Henry Esmond,* and *The Three Musketeers.* These I found unscientific and, except for certain technical details of the ancient institution of the tourney, intensely boring. With Rowena I was particularly disgusted, and the woman Beatrix furnished nothing to enlighten nor to admire.

"Imaginative trash," said my father; in which judgment I concurred, but mother had the last word.

"Nothing," she said, "has ever been accomplished until someone first dared imagine it. All scientific advance is based upon the daring imagination of some free mind."

The conversations that went on under our roof were not tempered to the ears of a child. In the main I listened to discussions far beyond my comprehension, but it was impossible that I should be otherwise than saturated with the constant downpour of science that beat upon me evening after evening. I fancy my vocabulary—for children pick up words from their seniors and fit them into their own mouths—was fantastic. I was more at home with learned jargon than I was with nursery tales. But, through no effort of my own and merely by contact, I came to understand a certain modicum of what assailed my ears.

As I look back I must have been a timorous urchin; certainly not one of the belligerent sort. 'Which brings me to Melinna, who appeared very briefly but importantly in my life, only to disappear for years even from my memory. And then to reappear most astoundingly, bringing with her occurrences shocking and perilous, which pushed me close to the abyss of being declared a traitor to my country.

She was a little fat girl of seven years when I encountered her first, and she was not yet eight years old when she vanished from my orbit. But upon me, a ten-year-old, she left her indelible mark. As, indeed, she must leave an indelible mark upon any with whom she comes in contact.

On the other side of the campus lived a boy of about my own age, but smaller and of unbelievable belligerence. For some reason he regarded me as his especial prey. Every time I ventured out of my own yard and into territory which he regarded as his own, he would emit aggressive and threatening whoops and chase me home to the refuge of my own fenced yard.

One morning—I had not reached my eleventh year at the time—I was returning from some errand when this juvenile enemy spied me and, with menacing shouts, bore down upon me. I turned tail and fled for home and the protection of my yard. I was outdistancing my pursuer, being fleet of foot, when I realized that I was being spoken to.

"Big sissy!" said a voice, and I became aware of a fat little girl swinging on a gate.

I slackened my flight a trifle, surprised but not humiliated by her accusation.

"He always—chases—me!" I panted.

"Stop," she said peremptorily, "and fight him, if you're not a ninny."

Quite astonishingly I thought of Rowena and the tournament at Ashbyde-la-Zouche, and the Queen of Love and Beauty, and the heralds shouting at the knights that fair eyes beheld their deeds. Never before had I imagined that such a scene could have a practical modern application. Nor was the fat little girl an individual one would select to be Queen of Love and Beauty. Nevertheless, a queer thing happened to me, which, perhaps, psychologists could explain. Flight became repugnant. Ivanhoe would not have skedaddled for home as I was doing. So

I halted, and quite without intending to do so, I found myself reversing direction and charging upon my tormentor. He was as surprised as I, and halted, and I collided with him so that he fell upon his back and I found myself sitting on his stomach. He started to bawl, and I was conscious of a curious elation that I never before had experienced. I sat astride of him and did not know what to do next.

The fat little girl leaned over the gate and yelled at me, not excitedly, but calmly. "Tell him to say 'uncle'," she directed.

"Say 'uncle'!" I commanded, though I did not know what saying that word would signify.

"Uncle," said my adversary tearfully.

"Now," said the chubby little girl, "let him up. You've licked him." I scrambled off my recumbent enemy, and he got to his feet and ran pell-mell down the street.

"Never let anybody chase you," the girl said severely. "Now you may come in and play with me."

"I don't want to play with you," I answered.

"Yes, you do," she said; "only you're too bashful."

I was very uncomfortable and embarrassed, and I knew my ears were red. I went away from there without looking back. She swung on her gate and called jeeringly after me, "Yaah! You'll be back, and then I won't play with you!"

As I look back over the years of my life—which are not many, because I am at this hour twenty-seven years of age—I become aware that this was a highly important event with a definite effect upon the formation of my character. It taught me, among other things, that individuals of the other sex may exercise an influence over one's actions that cannot be logically explained. It also taught me that it is more effective and, indeed, more enjoyable, to charge than it is to flee. For many days, rather than pass her house again, I would walk around the block.

I found, to my juvenile annoyance, that this chubby little girl exercised a peculiar attraction which seemed to me mingled with a repulsion. I wanted to have nothing to do with her, but at the same time I was drawn to her proximity. So I spied upon her from behind lilac bushes and fences and other suitable places of concealment, and derived little satisfaction from it.

One morning as I lay prone in a clump of rhododendrons, she came skipping in my direction and stopped and executed some sort of pirouette. I knew she was showing off, which meant that I had been discovered. "Come out," she said, "I know you're there, I knew you were there yesterday. You are a stupid boy."

"You," I retorted, "are a show-off."

She turned up her nose at me. "Everybody says," she jeered, "that your parents and your uncles and your aunts are raising you to be a juvenile prodigy. What's a juvenile prodigy? My uncle says you will probably turn out to be a dud."

"I am not any prodigy!" I said furiously. "My mother, who knows, says everything about me is normal but my environment, and she's going to see to it I rise superior to that."

"You talk like a nasty prodigy," she said. "Do you believe in space ships?"

"In what?"

"In an airship that can travel through space and go to Mars and Saturn and other planets, and fight with the wicked inhabitants, who have eight legs, and rescue the beautiful lavender-colored princess?"

"I never," said I, feeling very superior, "heard of such nonsense."

"It's in a book," she answered, as if that settled the matter. "You wait right here and I'll get the book."

Presently she returned with a volume and sat by while I read it. It was about a rocket ship that navigated interstellar space, and a boy who had strange adventures. I did not care greatly about the adventures, but the idea of a ship that could penetrate the earth's atmosphere and, relying upon jet propulsion, travel at enormous speeds through space to other planets fascinated me. The author of the book made it sound very logical and scientific and feasible.

"So there," said the girl. "If it's in a book it's so." She regarded me with a look in her eyes that made me very uncomfortable. "If you," she said, "are such a prodigy, you will invent a space ship and take me with you on voyages up—up there!" and she pointed to the sky.

"I'll invent a space ship," I said firmly, "but I won't take any girls along, you can bet."

"Then," she said, "you're nothing but a mean, selfish, nasty juvenile prodigy. And you'll probably end up cutting out paper dolls. My uncle says so."

Someone in her house called, "Puddin'," and she got up and went *away*. It was all the name I ever heard for her, at least for many years. I did not see her again. It seems she was a visitor in Professor Mason's—some kind of niece or something. And she went away. But for the second time in a week she had modified my life. She had aroused in me an interest in jet propulsion and the possibilities of navigating space beyond the earth's atmosphere which has not diminished, but on the contrary has increased to this day—to the extent that I have devoted my talents, such as they are, to the study of jet propulsion, guided missiles and electronic controls.

With the result that today, at the age of twenty-seven, having been investigated meticulously by the Federal Bureau of Investigation as to my loyalty to the United States of America, I am on my way westward to a place in the desert of New Mexico known as 'White Sands Proving Ground, there to aid, in a civilian capacity, in the development of rockets capable of exploring the atmosphere which surrounds the earth, and the space above it. And also to take part in experiments which may result in the production of a weapon of war which may be launched, say, in New Mexico, and guided by a robot electronic brain so exactly that, within a matter of minutes, it will reach the office in which the Kremlin bosses sit dictating the policies of Soviet Russia to the detriment of the world.

I am convinced by years of study that such a weapon, of such long range and accuracy, is now well within the bounds of scientific possibility. I am convinced that we are nearing the hour when a rocket, jet-propelled, carrying a crew of human beings, can be launched from Earth and reach a destination on Mars.

Of that much I am definitely convinced. But an integral and important part of the problem will remain. As I say, I am convinced that we can overcome difficulties of speed, heat, atmosphere or the lack of it, and arrive on the surface of Mars. But for the life of me, I cannot discover any method by which that rocket could be relaunched and made to return to Earth. "Which, as all will admit, would give pause to anyone thinking of enlisting as a member of the rocket's crew.

My life has been rather on the monastic side, so that my experience with women, save laboratory assistants and others living more or less devoted lives, has been negligible. I may say that I have been practically unconscious of women as members of another sex.

The young woman who sat next me in the club car of the Golden State Limited was unmistakably of another sex. She seemed to make a point of advertising that fact. She clothed herself in such a manner as to call to one's attention the contours of her person, and her movements and postures only emphasized the purely animal character of her femininity. When you looked at her, when you were in her proximity, you were not merely conscious of another human being but that the human being was female. This was made more noticeable by the faint odor of perfume which emanated from her.

She was of medium height, I judged, and slender, but by no means emaciated. I found myself looking at her surreptitiously with something more than the normal disinterest which one bestows upon strangers. Indeed, I found it impossible to keep my eyes away from her. She, also, seemed to be surveying me.

"You," she said unexpectedly, "are a big man." She almost said "beeg man," with the merest trace of foreign accent.

I furnished her with statistics. "I am," I told her, "six feet and one inch in height, and my weight is a hundred and ninety-eight pounds."

"So it should be," she observed—"big and strong, but not bulging."

"I do not bulge," I said firmly.

"It is an evident thing," she agreed. "You are perhaps a

famous athlete?"

"I am a scientist," I informed her.

"But in such condition!" she exclaimed. "Such fitness."

"Mens sana in corpora sano," I observed.

"But naturally," she rejoined. "What science is yours?"

"I am," said I, "presently engaged in electronic research as it bears upon rocket vehicles."

"Oh!" she exclaimed, wide-eyed. "To fly to the moon!"

"So far," I said, "our success has fallen somewhat short of that. It is measured by hundreds of miles rather than millions."

"And you have gone so high!" she exclaimed with manifest admiration.

"No one," I said, "has ascended so high." I spoke austerely because I have little patience with persons who discuss topics of which they have no knowledge.

"My name," she said unexpectedly, "is Renee du Guesclin."

"Mine," I responded politely, "is Thomas Alva Edison Gimp."

"So now," she smiled at me, "we are introduced, is it not?"

"We have exchanged names," said I, "which is quite a different matter."

"How different?" she asked.

"An introduction," said I, "presupposes a sponsor for one person or the other—a common acquaintance who, in effect, makes himself responsible in presenting one person to another. He performs an act in which, tacitly, he guarantees the characters and backgrounds and integrity of the two strangers involved. We have only named our names, with no one to guarantee our respectability."

"How very formal you are," she said. "Now, I am not formal at all."

"Formality," said I, "is but another name for rules of behavior that have stood the test of time and experience."

"Me," she said, making a little grimace, "I like to break rules."

Although I would have preferred that she desist from annoying me with bootless conversation, she showed no signs of doing so. She was a chattering woman. "I," she said, "would like to fly to Mars."

"In heaven's name, why?" I asked with some impatience. "If, with your untrained mind, you reached the planet Mars and returned, your observations would be without value to science."

"Must everything you do have a value?"

"Yes," said I.

"I think that is nonsense," she said. "You do things for fun or for excitement. I love to do things that are exciting. Don't you ever do things just for fun or excitement?"

"Never," said I. "Definitely not for excitement. When one becomes excited he loses his mental balance."

"I have found that to be just dandy. The loveliest things happen when you lose your mental balance—when it is the heart that takes control and not the mind."

"The heart," said I, "is a mere piece of mechanism whose chief function is to propel blood through the veins and arteries. How can a—a piece of meat control the reason?"

"So that," she asked, tilting her head sidewise, "is your idea of the business of a heart?"

"Precisely," I rejoined.

She shook her head. "You are so very learned," she told me, "but you are so very ignorant." She moved her head up and down three times in an emphatic way. "It would be fun to teach you."

"Fun," said I.

"Have you ever been in love, professor? Or is it doctor?"

"Doctor," said I. "An earned and not an honorary degree. Definitely I never have been in love. It is a loose term which describes a romantic impossibility. I credit the existence of affection, for I have experienced it. I credit the existence of physical passion, because it is a biological essential. But love! One of your writers of romance, named, I believe, J. M. Barrie, once defined love. He said it was a mixture of affection and passion sanctioned by Divine Providence for the perpetuation of mankind. Loose and unscientific, but nevertheless conveying an idea."

"How silly!" she exclaimed. "Love is for itself. It is to be enjoyed for itself. It is an emotion that produces ecstasy."

"And what," I demanded tartly, "is ecstasy?"

"Ecstasy," she said, "is what makes you cease to be a mere human being and transports you into a world where dwell only gods and goddesses." Suddenly she smiled. "Ecstasy is riding on one of your jet-propelled rockets into interplanetary space."

"This," said I, "is a strange conversation."

"I," she retorted, "am a strange woman."

I became aware that the man across from us—the one who looked more like a romanticized statue of a man—was listening with a smile of amusement. He was a big man, as large as myself. His clothing was the perfection of tailoring. His hair was not white with age, for he seemed in his early thirties, but of that shade to which women refer as platinum. And it waved in a manner that made you think he devoted attention to its care. Like a Greek statue, he had no bridge to his nose. He was by no means a flamboyant figure, but he was distinctly noticeable. His smile, as our eyes met, was ironical. His glance caused me a slight embarrassment, and I turned my eyes away.

In the second seat from him sat an older man, who might have reached his fortieth year. He was not Anglo-Saxon. I took him to be a member of one of the southern races, with his liquid brown eyes and olive complexion. Something about his gray suit informed me that it had not been tailored in the United States. I hazarded a guess that he was a citizen of the republic south of the Rio Grande. He, too, was peering at me, but without amusement, indeed with the hint of a frown. His was a very acute face, with resolute jaw. It seemed to me that my conversation with Miss du Guesclin was causing the two gentlemen amusement on the part of one and distaste on the part of the other.

Miss du Guesclin commanded my attention. "I am hungry," she said. "Shall we go in to dinner?"

It seemed to me that this suggestion was not warranted by anything that had preceded it; indeed that it was forward. But

I did not know how to repulse her. She arose and preceded me, walking sinuously, so that one became aware of her hips and of the swaying of them. I did not realize until we reached the dining car that the two gentlemen across the aisle had arisen as we did, and were upon our heels. In the diner there was only one vacant table, which seated four persons. The steward conducted Miss du Guesclin and me to it and seated us facing forward. The two gentlemen appropriated the seats opposite us. Each of them bowed—a courtesy which I returned. We addressed ourselves to the menu and ordered.

I was attracted by the appearance of the man whom I took to be Mexican. He moved gracefully, was slender, but giving the appearance of wiry strength. I was not attracted by the other man, nor by his massiveness or the artificiality of his appearance.

"What time," asked the Mexican of me, "do we reach Kansas City?" It was, doubtless, a mere polite manner of dispelling any awkwardness that might exist. I informed him of the hour of our arrival at that city.

"Am I," he asked, "mistaken in identifying you as Doctor Gimp?"

"That," said I, "is my name."

"It is an honor," he said, "to be dining with a scientist of such eminence."

It was effusive, and I do not know how to cope with effusiveness. It flusters me. I mumbled an inappropriate reply. The other man then spoke. "I," he said, "am Doctor Balthasar Toledo."

"Indeed," said I. "Medicine?"

"Fine arts," he replied. He smiled, and I must admit his smile was not without charm. "I'm supposed," he said, "to be quite a dabster in Renaissance paintings. If someone deals for a Titian, I tell him if it is genuine."

"And I," said the Mexican, "am Senor Iturbe, of Mexico City. A mere man of business."

This seemed to require that I introduce Miss du Guesclin, which I did with some reluctance.

"You are going to the Coast, doctor?" asked Toledo.

"I alight at El Paso," I informed him.

"Ah, yes. Ah, yes. I should have guessed. On your way to White Sands?"

"On my way to 'White Sands," I answered.

"A tremendous work they are doing. Which may have profound effect upon the future of the world."

Senor Iturbe was peering at me intently, brows knitted. I had a feeling that he was striving to convey a message of caution. It was not necessary.

I am not one to babble secrets, even though I may be in many ways a guileless man of science. I have found that one way to discourage curiosity and to preserve secrecy upon matters best not discussed is to seem eruditely garrulous.

"Yes, indeed," I answered. "We are now enabled to explore not only the troposphere, which is our ordinary atmosphere extending upward some seven or eight miles, but the stratosphere, which reaches approximately to sixty miles, and the ionosphere, with extends thence to interplanetary space. Into these various areas we send rocket and balloon vehicles which are, in effect, flying laboratories, carrying observing and recording instruments such as cameras, radios, spectographs, Geiger counters, cloud chambers, which make and place on available records most significant scientific data."

"How fascinating!" exclaimed Miss du Guesclin.

I continued to be garrulous, hoping to increase their boredom. "These vehicles furnish hitherto inaccessible information as to the meteorology of the upper air, cosmic radiation and spectroscopy, including valuable data of importance in rocket propulsion, aerodynamics, and so forth and so on."

Senor Iturbe's eyes twinkled, and he relaxed visibly. I found difficulty in restraining myself from winking at him, but deemed it undignified. Then I asked myself why I should share a humorous little understanding with this man, and what business was it of his, anyway.

Here I was, an unaccustomed traveler, involved with three individuals whom I never had seen before, and whom I had no desire to see again. In this I was to be appallingly disappointed. I am no believer in fate or destiny, but there are moments when I can sympathize with those who hold those superstitions. One could, upon the experiences which lay just ahead of me, establish a *prima facie* case for predestination, particularly in the astonishing appearance, or rather reappearance, of Melinna.

I did find some mild amusement in the situation. It was apparent to me that the art expert, Balthasar Toledo, wished to lead me into conversation about White Sands and the topic of guided missiles. His interest was not in the exploration of the heavens and the research to be carried on there for the benefit of mankind, but rather in the use of rockets in warfare. But I made pretense that that phase of the matter did not interest me. Each time he propounded a question, I evaded it by launching a spate of scientific jargon, tossing in such words as "tropopause," to indicate that line at which temperature ceases to drop at the rate of a degree for each three hundred feet of altitude and becomes constant, and "ion concentration" and "exosphere," where the ionosphere commences to merge with interplanetary space. All this bored him dreadfully, so that his one desire was to dam my freshet of incomprehensible terminology. I took impish delight in his evident boredom.

Even Miss du Gucsclin ceased to ply me with her undoubtedly potent animal attributes, and yawned. We finished dessert hurriedly and, in the club car, I said good night and made my way to my bedroom, which I had some difficulty in locating. I always experience this minor vexation. Each time I seek my quarters for the night on a train it is a lesser adventure, usually terminating in my having to demand the assistance of some uniformed official in leading me to my bed.

IT IS my habit to arise early, so I breakfasted without encountering my acquaintances of the night before. I returned speedily to my compartment where I occupied myself pleasantly reading a paper by Doctor Griffith, of Yale University.

I ventured forth again at noon, but was not molested,

though I sat in the club car for an hour. Miss du Guesclin did not appear, nor Doctor Toledo, nor Senor Iturbe, the least objectionable member of the trio.

It would not be long now until I arrived at my destination, El Paso; so I arose and moved toward my compartment to see that my impedimenta were packed and secured, and that I did not, according to my custom, debark from the train leaving behind pajamas or toilet articles. This time I moved surely and without bewilderment, and confidently opened a door off the passageway. My own quarters were Bedroom E in Car 426. The door that I opened and entered so surely was Bedroom E in Car 425, as I subsequently discovered.

I was disgruntled to find someone sprawled upon the seat which at night was made into my berth.

"I beg your pardon!" I said severely.

The man did not move, I entered farther, and was able to identify the intruder. It was Senor Iturbe, and something was wrong with him. The thing that was wrong with him was that the handle of a knife protruded from his back, and I did not need to make a more detailed examination to be informed that he was dead.

It was my first encounter with violent death, and I was appalled. Nevertheless, I am pleased to note that panic did not seize me and that I did not conduct myself in an unseemly manner. I retreated into the corridor. At the end of the car, a porter sat drowsing, and I summoned him.

He came to me and I stood aside so that he could look into the bedroom.

"There has," I said, "been a murder. Summon the conductor at once."

His eyes rolled and his skull took on a grayish tinge. He scurried away and I took the precaution to close the door, so that the interior of the room would be concealed from the eyes of passers-by. In a matter of minutes the porter returned with the conductor, and with a thin young man in a neat blue suit.

"'What's this? What's this?" the conductor demanded.

"A gentleman," said I—calmly, I believe—"has been murdered. His name is Iturbe."

"You discovered him, Doctor Gimp?" the young man in the blue suit asked. "How?"

"I," I answered, "blundered into the wrong bedroom." Somewhat shamefacedly, I added, "I have a way of getting lost on trains."

His eyes twinkled momentarily; then he opened the door and entered the little cubicle, where he stood looking down upon the body. Then he turned to me. "Doctor," he asked, "do you think you can find your own bedroom?"

"I'm sure I can," I replied.

"Then," he directed, "You will please go to it and remain there until I come for you. You will mention this to no one."

"I hope I will not be detained as a witness," I said. "I should get to my destination without delay."

"You will not be detained," he answered. "You will reach White Sands without delay."

"You know my name and my destination."

"So it would seem," he said with a smile. "Now, if you please, be so good as to dissociate yourself from this unpleasant affair promptly. I will come for you when we reach El Paso."

I withdrew and walked to the next car, which was the correct one, and entered my bedroom. It would be an untruth to state that I was not shaken or that I was not bewildered by the turn of events. The young man in the blue suit knew my name and destination; he seemed to desire that I should not be involved in the murder of Sailor Iturbe. Though he wore no outward insigne of authority, he seemed to have taken command of the situation, and the conductor made no objection. I wondered who and what he could be.

I completed the packing of my belongings and sat staring out of the window until we reached the outskirts of the city of El Paso and drew into the station. There came a knock upon my door, and I opened it. The young man in the blue suit stood there.

"Ready?" he asked.

"Quite ready," I said.

"Your baggage checks, please." He extended his hand and I gave him the check to my trunk. He accompanied me off the train, took my suitcase and escorted me into the station. There at the information desk waited a young man in the uniform of a private in the United States Army.

"For Doctor Gimp?" my companion asked.

"Yes, sir," the soldier said.

"You have a car?"

"Yes, sir."

This time the soldier took my suitcase and we walked out of the building to a military car that awaited at the curb. The young man in the blue suit extended his hand with a grin.

"I think you'll get there all right now," he said, "without blundering into anything else. . . . Keep an eye on the doctor," he said to the soldier.

"Yes, sir," answered the boy.

"Thank you. You have been very helpful," I said.

"Thanks are quite unnecessary," he smiled. "I earn my living this way." We drove out of the city, through a huge military installation, which my driver informed me was Fort Bliss, and out into the desert.

"We'll have to take the long way," he said. "The roads are closed on the short cut."

"Why?" I asked.

"They're shooting off things today," he answered.

We proceeded at a rapid gait through desert terrain that bristled with military signs warning the tourist. At last we came to a tiny roadside structure from which emerged a young man in a well-fitting gray-blue uniform. We alighted and went inside with him, where I signed things and was given a card to identify me.

A young woman sat in a chair in the corner. As the formalities were completed, she arose and came toward us.

"Hello, Peter," she said to the soldier. "You're my transportation."

"Glad to have you, Miss Brown," he said, and then rather awkwardly, "Miss Brown, this is Doctor Gimp."

She gave me a small hand. "We've been expecting you," she said, and gave me an odd little sidewise look. "I'm a laboratory assistant."

"Charmed," I said mechanically, giving her the barest glance. It sufficed to show me that she was a tiny person with brown hair and eyes, slender, with a piquant face which might almost be characterized as mischievous.

We went out and I helped her into the car and took my place beside her. I sat back, having no conversation to make, and looked ahead. My eyes rested on the instrument board of the car. Stenciled on the metal above it was an admonition:

THIS VEHICLE COST $1,150. DRIVE CAREFULLY.

"Is this your first visit to 'White Sands?" Miss Brown asked.

"My first."

"Then," she said, "to make conversation I'll tell you that this Army Ordnance proving ground is forty miles wide and a hundred miles long. Ninety miles north of headquarters is the place where the first atomic bomb was touched off. Alamogordo is about forty miles away, and Las Cruces, over the Organ Mountains yonder, is twenty-six miles. There are about two thousand civilians working here, and a couple of thousand soldiers. Maybe seven hundred women, which isn't enough to go around. A good many civilian employees live in El Paso and Las Cruces, and commute. The food is middling and the recreation doesn't make you turn flip-flops. It's hotter than hell's hinges in summer, and colder than a snake's heart in winter. Anything else?"

"You chatter," I said firmly.

"It makes me a social asset," she said.

"Not with me," I replied.

"Wait," she said, "until you've been here a month, and I'll grow on you."

"I shall have no time for diversions or for women."

"Doctor," she said gravely, "the time is not long distant, in this arid country, when even a female scorpion will have its attractions."

I assumed an expression of austerity intended to discourage further feminine dithering. She became demure and fell silent. After a mile or two of this, I was conscious of a species of social discomfort, and found it necessary to speak.

"You wear a badge," said I.

"Everybody wears badges," she said. "Security. We're nuts on security. We're classified. Some get a badge that entitles them to breathe. Some get a badge that entitles them to open their eyes after sunup. Some get a badge that entitles them to go through gates, and some a badge that lets them enter doors. This one," she said, touching the oblong affixed to her left breast, "is the real aristocrat of badges. It entitles you to know all, to see all, to go anywhere, and to keep your trap shut. You'll have one like it."

"Indeed," I said.

Ahead, buildings became visible. I saw in a battery installations for the cameras that photographed missiles in flight. To the right was a structure whose flat roof bristled with the bowl-like disks of a radar installation. Miss Brown indicated the building.

"That," she said, "is as full of miracles as a girl's head is of romance."

"An absurd simile," said I.

"Can you think of anything fuller?" she demanded.

"The heads of girls," said I, "are quite outside my field of research."

Then she said an odd thing that touched a chord of memory. It was only a faint, elusive vibration, not then to be identified by me, but disturbing.

"They," she said tartly, "did succeed in raising a prodigy." And then, "They might, as an afterthought, have added a pinch of normal this and that to the prescription."

To this, I responded nothing, setting it down as mere feminine gibberish.

"But it may not be too late," she said.

We now approached the cluster of buildings and drew up before broad steps which climbed to the entrance to past headquarters.

"Colonel Ramsay," she said, "is on the second floor, third office to the left." She grinned in an irritating way. "I looked in the crystal ball," she said. "It says we'll be seeing each other."

"I doubt it," I responded.

"Peter," she said, "will take me to the lab. Then he'll come back and cart you to your lodging for the night."

"Good afternoon," I said formally. I alighted and entered the building, where I went through the formalities of being inducted into the intricate life of White Sands. I received my badge, from which I must never be parted, was instructed to report in the morning to Doctor Newcomb, at the laboratory, and was then driven to my quarters for the night in what I took to be a sort of officers' club.

Peter carried my baggage to the room assigned to me. I bathed, changed my linen, and suddenly was overcome by a feeling of loneliness combined with claustrophobia. I put on my hat and strolled out into the late afternoon sunshine.

I had not reached the road when a car stopped and a slender, wiry officer alighted. He wore the insignia of an Army major.

"Doctor Gimp?" he asked.

"I am he," said I.

He extended a hand which gripped mine with firmness. His shrewd gray eyes surveyed me so that I felt he was acquainting himself with the exact position of every button of my clothing and every freckle on my face. His smile was pleasant, but a trifle grim.

"I," he said, "am Major Van Tuyl, chief of intelligence and security."

"Delighted," I said courteously.

"You may not be," he answered.

"And why not, sir?"

"Because," he said, "I sometimes ask people to do disagreeable things."

"Such as?" I inquired.

"In your case," he replied, "not living at ease in quarters assigned to you here."

"I do not understand."

"You don't need to understand," he said abruptly. "I cannot order you. I can only make the request."

"What request, sir?"

"That you live in El Paso and commute to the laboratory twice a day.

There are buses."

"It seems an unnecessary hardship."

"Let me be the judge of necessity," he said. "A comfortable apartment will be provided you in El Paso."

"And what do I do there, Major?"

"Nothing," he answered.

"Then," said I, "your request seems absurd."

He smiled again, and in a friendly manner. " 'They also serve,' " he quoted, " 'who only stand and wait.' "

"For what do I wait?"

"Maybe," he said grimly, "for nothing. Maybe for all hell to break loose."

"I am a scientist," said I, "not a man of action. I would not know how to conduct myself if all hell should break loose."

He surveyed me again and grinned. "You've got the size and weight for it," he observed. "Boys who were not accustomed to it died in Asia."

"I've no ambition to die."

"And we," he said, "have every ambition to keep you alive."

"Let me understand," said I. "You are requesting, not ordering, me to occupy an apartment in El Paso?"

"Precisely."

"Which," I continued, "may involve me in the breaking loose, as you express it, of hell?"

"Exactly," he said.

"To what end?" I asked.

"Even though you are immersed in scientific research," he said, "I take it you are not unaware of unrest in the world."

"It has come to my attention," I said dryly.

"Also," he said, "that you might be willing to be of service to your country in ways we might call extra-scientific."

"I," said I, "am not without veneration for this republic."

"So I imagined after reading your dossier."

"What will I be required to do in El Paso?"

"Lead a normal life. Do not avoid people who show a desire to make your acquaintance. Simply be yourself."

Now I am also not without a rudimentary intelligence in matters outside the field of science. The idea was penetrating. For some reason he wished me to take upon myself the role of bait for some sort of quarry.

I shrugged and smiled at him.

"Do you read Kipling?" I asked.

"I know him almost by memory."

"Then," said I, "you will recall the quotation. I think it is to be found in *Stalky and Company:* 'The bleating of the kid excites the tiger.' "

Now he grinned broadly. "I take it you will be willing to be the kid?"

"But with no keen desire," said I, "to excite the tiger."

"If you should," he said, "there will be a hunter up a nearby tree who is an excellent marksman."

"Very well," I said. "But I hope your hunter does not run out of ammunition at the crucial moment."

He extended his hand. "Obliged," he said. "Now suppose we forget all about it and have dinner at the officers' club."

"I greatly fear," said I, "that you have ruined my appetite."

Part Two

I AWOKE early and had breakfast in the pleasant dining room at a surprisingly reasonable price. A number of young naval officers were seated at a common table with me. They greeted me courteously and without curiosity to see a civilian among their fresh uniforms. I finished my breakfast and was just leaving the dining room when a tall, stooping gentleman with an intelligent, arresting face came in from outside and mentioned my name to the attendant. I approached him.

"Doctor Gimp?" he inquired, extending a hand.

"Doctor Newcomb," I responded.

"Welcome to White Sands," he said with real cordiality. "We've been needing you."

"I hope I shall not be valueless," I replied.

He conducted me to the door. "I thought it possible," he said, "that you might like to orient yourself. I have a car. I would be delighted to show you about our metropolis."

He drove me about the not inconsiderable area, pointing out various buildings and naming their functions. We passed an athletic field, a theater, a chapel. We saw the Navy's swimming pool, and the laboratory with its imposing entrance, and the bank, and the dispensary. There were mess hall, clubs for enlisted men and officers, and on the outskirts hard by the housing area a number of house trailers huddling together.

"All three services are represented," said Doctor Newcomb, "Army, Navy and Air." He grinned. "They live very peacefully and co-operate. No need to drive out to the launching sites," he said. "We'll be going out there this afternoon. Army's going to launch some rockets. You'll want to see that."

We covered the immediate area thoroughly, and then alighted at the laboratory, where Doctor Newcomb showed me the room that was to be mine and conducted me over the premises. A civilian guard in gray-blue uniform, with a pistol on his hip, guarded the outer door and scrutinized our badges skeptically, even though Doctor Newcomb was so well acquainted with him as to call him Paddy.

"Security," the doctor grinned. "These guards are all ex-servicemen. Theirs not to reason why, theirs but to stop everybody at every door and gate. Won't even let a dog through without a badge, lest it carry subversive fleas."

I was, of course, introduced to various colleagues, who were gracious and whose names I would have to catalogue and remember. In the corridor I passed Miss Brown, who grinned at the doctor and then eyed me mischievously.

"So you caught up with the prodigy," she said gaily. "He's going to give our social life a shot in the arm. I rode in with him yesterday. He's a wolf, doctor. You wouldn't think it to look at him, but he's a ravening wolf. I didn't draw a long breath till I got out of the car."

"I," said I stiffly, "do not know why I should be referred to as other than a human being."

"Miss Brown," said the doctor, his eyes twinkling, "gives off reactions."

"Which," said I, "I trust will not come within my purview."

She turned her head to one side and peered up at me impertinently. "That," she replied, "I am taking under consideration."

She passed on her way, and Doctor Newcomb and I sat down in his office for a necessary conference. He sat behind his desk and looked at me slantwise. "Just how," he asked, "did you ruffle Miss Brown's feathers?"

"I'm sure I do not know. I tried to ignore her."

"Ah," he said, and nodded, "One does not ignore Miss Brown."

We spent the remainder of the morning in agreeable technical conversation, after which we went to lunch in the officers' club. Some time after our return we were driven out to a launching site. Again we were stopped at a gate by a civilian guard whom we had to satisfy as to our right to pass. Off to our right I saw an enormous gantry crane, a huge skeleton of steel with platforms which could be lowered within its arch to work upon such enormous rockets as the Viking or the German V-2 while they were in vertical position before discharge.

Just ahead of us was a massive launching-control building, commonly called a blockhouse, constructed of concrete, its roof in the shape of a truncated pyramid. For the safety of those working inside, this roof is a solid block twenty-seven feet in thickness.

Scattered about were various vehicles, camera stations, trucks for the transportation of rockets, and off to the left were two slender vicious white projectiles on their launching platforms. These did not point directly upward, as do the larger rockets before launching, but lay at an angle, their sharp noses in the direction of the proposed flight. Their purpose was to be discharged from a fixed base at a target which was also upon the surface of the earth or the water.

More to the right I perceived a smaller, slenderer guided missile denominated "Nike." It reclined on its carriage ready to be moved at a later time into launching position.

We walked across the concrete area and entered the blockhouse. Here was a room whose walls seemed to be lined with steel filing cases, but these, upon examination, proved to be a battery or batteries of electronic devices for receiving and recording information returning from the rocket in flight or from other recording devices located in stations along the line of flight.

Before us was a block of glass, facing toward the launching area. It was many inches thick, but so clear that one could see through it easily.

Behind this window we stationed ourselves. Across the intervening space we could see a number of men preparing the two rockets for their impending flight.

The wait seemed interminable, but at last a man was sent outside to discharge a warning flare. Then, over the loudspeaker, a voice commenced to count in reverse, "Twenty . . . nineteen . . . eighteen . . . seventeen"—ticking off the seconds. The number diminished: "Seven . . . six . . . five . . . four . . . three . . . two . . . one."

Tension built up within us. As the last second vanished into the past, there was a tremendous flare of almost unbearable light and an almost simultaneous blast of sound. It was not an explosion, but a Gargantuan whoosh which seemed bent upon tearing out the eardrums. We strained our eyes. Objects became visible, but the rocket was gone. In the air remained nothing but wisps of vapor. The great projectile had vanished into the void.

The incredible force and velocity of the missile were appalling. It also passed almost beyond the bounds of credulity that there existed an instrument here capable of registering and of reporting upon its flight; that it itself might be sending back messages from the electronic devices concealed in its interior, recording its experiences as if they were written down by a human hand in a diary.

"Everything lovely," said Doctor Newcomb. He chuckled. "Not always so. We launched a captured German V-2 not so long ago. It started its flight, and when it got up a little way it turned eccentric. It cut off at right angles and headed for Mexico. Next we heard of it, it had plumped down in a graveyard across the border. No harm done."

We waited for the launching of the second rocket and drove back to the laboratory, where a message awaited me asking me to telephone Major Van Tuyl. I did so, and was promptly connected with the chief of intelligence and security.

"If it's agreeable," he said, "we're driving you to El Paso this evening, with your baggage. Want to get you safely settled."

"The attractive word in that sentence," said I, "is 'safely.' "

I could hear his chuckle. "When shall the car come for you?" he asked. "I'm ready now," I answered.

PRESENTLY my baggage was placed in the rear of the car and I was on my way to the Texas border city. There was the driver, of course, but sitting in the back seat with me was a young man who introduced himself as Mr. Martin. He wore a neat blue suit and rather resembled the young man whom I had met on the train and who had unexpectedly taken charge of my affairs until I was safely ensconced in a motorcar on my way to White Sands.

"Would you," I asked, "be one of Major Van Tuyl's security personnel?"

"No," he said. "I'm a special agent, FBI. We co-operate. White Sands works directly with our field office in Albuquerque. But this time a little help from El Paso seemed to be indicated."

Upon our arrival in El Paso I was conducted to a modest but pleasant apartment house. My quarters consisted of living room, bedroom and kitchenette, whose larder had been supplied with breakfast necessities.

"Satisfactory?" asked my companion.

"Completely," I answered. We sat down and he smoked. I am not a user of tobacco.

"May I ask," said I, "what is expected of me?"

"Nothing," he said. "just go ahead and behave in a perfectly normal manner."

"The criticism has been facetiously made of me," said I, "that I never behave in a so-called normal manner."

He grinned amiably. "In that case," he said, "behave in any eccentric manner you choose. . . . You will find a reasonably good dining room in this building." He arose, extended his hand and said, "Nice to have met you, doctor."

"Shall I be seeing you, sir?" I asked.

"That," he replied, "depends."

"Upon what?" I asked.

"Whether," he said, "the fish are taking flies or worms or grasshoppers."

I found myself alone. I spent some time in arranging my not extensive wardrobe and the few books I had brought with me. Then I bathed, shaved and took the elevator down to the dining room.

I dined heartily and fared forth to stroll about this strange and doubtless interesting city. I walked at random and after an interval found myself in the business heart of El Paso, a brightly lighted area of stores, hotels and places of amusement.

I paused to peer through a show window at a display of

devices calculated to ameliorate the labors of the housewife, such as machines for the washing of dishes, or the cleansing of clothes, or the beating of eggs, and reflected that the business of living seemed on the verge of becoming largely a matter of turning electric switches. I wondered if the race would learn to utilize wisely the leisure resulting from its mechanization.

As I turned away from this display I became aware of the approach of a young woman whose lithe movements, especially the sway of the hips, were vaguely familiar. One could not but be aware of the mechanical perfection of her body and of the smoothly synchronized movements of its several parts. One sees such excellence of design and such economy of efficient movement in many intricate mechanisms.

My eyes traveled upward from the lower members to her face, and I recognized, with no enthusiasm, the young person who had sat beside me in the club car of the Golden State Limited, and who had given her name as Renee du Guesclin.

"Why, Doctor Gimp!" she exclaimed. "How unexpected!"

"Neither expected nor unexpected," said I. "A mere negligible encounter."

"Oh, no, indeed!" she said. "I found you so interesting, doctor. It seemed too bad that we should merely meet briefly and never see each other again."

"I doubt," said I, "if we should find common interests."

"You," she replied with gravity, "are an attractive man. I am not a hideous woman. Does not that establish a common interest?"

"You refer, I suppose," said I, "to the attraction of sex?"

She looked up at me oddly and not without surprise. "Doctor," she said with an enigmatic smile, speaking with the merest trace of foreign accent, "eet is to be observed that you do not beat about bushes, but come at once to the point."

I lifted my hat. "Good evening, Miss du Guesclin," I said with intentional abruptness.

I turned away to proceed on my way. As I did so I heard a cry of pain and faced her again. "Oh," she said faintly, "I have turn' my ankle."

"A difficult thing to do," said I, "when one is standing still."

She seemed about to fall, and quite naturally I extended a supporting hand. She clung to me.

"You," she said pleadingly, "must get for me a taxicab! You must help me to my home!"

It was an appeal I found myself unable to refuse. After a short delay, I managed to attract the attention of the driver of a cab, and then half carried, half supported Miss du Guesclin to a seat within it. I was interested to note that I found this contact with her person not unpleasant. It would seem that there are reactions and emotions which affect the individual quite independently of intellect, and contrary to the dictates of reason.

Miss du Guesclin gave an address to the taxi driver and sat back in her corner, holding her ankle in her hands as if it pained her. Her distress caused her to forget that perfect modesty upon which our mothers and grandmothers set such store. I mean to say that quite naively and innocently her posture displayed a considerable area of her lower limbs and that, in the dim light, I had to be quite resolute to avert my eyes from the spectacle.

There was no conversation. Miss du Guesclin evinced a silent fortitude, uttering no exclamation indicative of pain. The cab came to a stop before a low white house of the variety known as a ranch house, and I helped the young lady out. Her disability to walk was more pronounced, and she leaned heavily upon me as we mounted the steps and arrived at the door. She fumbled in her bag and produced a key which she handed to me. I inserted it in the keyhole and opened the door. The hallway was lighted, as was a living room at the left.

"In there, please," she said, and I assisted her to a chair, into which she lowered herself, assuming much the same position as had been hers in the cab. There was this difference: the light was much better and my standing at a slight distance supplied a superior vantage point.

"Should I," I asked, "summon a physician?"

"No, no. Eef you will just help to remove the shoe."

I was embarrassed by this request, but it was an emergency to which I must respond. I knelt and somewhat awkwardly removed her shoe.

"There seems," said I, "to be no swelling."

"Already," she said, "it feels better."

"In that case," said I, "I will bid you good evening."

"But not yet! I have not thank' you. I have not offer' hospitality. You Americans! Always Scotch and soda."

"When I drink," said I, "I prefer beer, but I am not thirsty."

"Nonsense," she said peremptorily. "I, too, love beer. You will find it in the icebox. The kitchen is through the dining room yonder."

"But—" I protested.

"In the icebox," she repeated.

I could see no way of extricating myself. I determined to sip one glass of the beverage and abruptly take my departure. While I was absent I heard the telephone jangle, and when I returned, Miss du Guesclin had hobbled across the room to the instrument.

It was a brief conversation, of which, of course, I could hear but one side.

"Yes," she said, "it is I."

There was a pause while the individual at the other end of the line spoke. She replied testily, "I know my business."

There was another silence. Again Miss du Guesclin spoke, "Definitely roped," she said. I considered this to be cryptic. "Like," she went on, "snatching candy from a baby. . . . Enough. Good night."

She hobbled back to her chair. Somehow she managed to make the uneven gait attractive.

"Is it not a pleasant house?" she asked.

"My impression was," said I, "that you were traveling to the Coast."

"But not!" she exclaimed. "This is the house of a friend. It was lent to me. You like?"

"It seems habitable," I assured her.

"If," said she, "you would rub my ankle."

"Definitely not," I replied.

"It does not bite," she observed.

"It is a familiarity," said I, "which only your inexperience would suggest."

"And you," she said, "you have thees experience?"

"Certainly not," said I.

She shrugged. "What do you in El Paso? I thought White Sands."

"I shall live here," said I, "and commute."

"How lovely," she said, displaying pleasure. "We shall be neighbors. That is good. The evenings are long when one is alone. You will be lonely. I will be lonely. It is a coincidence."

"I shall not be lonely," said I.

She smiled very prettily. "Then," she said, "you will take pity on me, no?"

"No," said I.

"That," she stated, "we shall see."

I arose and moved toward the door.

"Must you go?" she asked.

"It is not," said I, "a matter of compulsion, but of preference."

"Such beeg words," she said, indicating by holding her hands far apart. "Oh, I have such ignorance. You could teach me so much. I think," she said with a little *moue*, "I should learn so fast."

"I am not," I said austerely, "a tutor for young ladies."

She smiled up at me very charmingly. "Perhaps," she said, "the young lady could be a tutor for you. . . . If it must be so, then good night, doctor. You will come again soon?"

"Neither," said I, "soon nor late."

She laughed outright, as at some witticism. "That we shall see," she said, and extended her hand, which nestled in my own warmly. It seemed to express something which I could not translate. Nevertheless, the sensation was not unpleasant.

It was my intention, after a somewhat fatiguing day, to return to my apartment and retire immediately. But this, my first evening in El Paso, was not to terminate so uneventfully. It remained for me to make yet another acquaintance in somewhat absurd and bizarre circumstances.

I walked at my usual deliberate pace for a couple of blocks and was descending a street which tilted downward not sharply, but noticeably. My thoughts were turned inward, appraising the conduct of Miss du Guesclin toward myself; considering it from a coldly scientific point of view. The conclusion I reached, based upon such data as were available, was that the young lady was singularly frank and naive, and unacquainted with the ways of the world to the point where she was overtrusting in her attitude toward strangers such as myself. Her desire for friendship and companionship was pathetic. Had it not been for her undoubted pulchritude, I might have responded in kind, but I am well aware of the dangers involved in association with beauty. No man is impervious. Much as my sympathy flowed out to her, I determined firmly not to involve myself.

Having arrived at this wise decision, I turned my mind to other reflections of a historical nature involving popular misconception that the rocket in warfare is a new development. It is an indisputable fact that the rocket was known to the Chinese nearly five thousand years ago. Later history reveals that it was used as a weapon of war in A.D. 1232 in their defense of the city of Pien-King. That mysterious and learned man, Roger Bacon, had news of this and wrote of it in 1249, and it was speedily adopted in Europe to the point that rockets secured the victory for their users at the Battle of Chiozza in 1379. Rockets were considered more accurate than the crude artillery of the day. A venturesome Chinese inventor of the fifteenth century, named Wan-Hoo, essayed a flight through the air propelled by these missiles. Quite unwisely, but with boldness, he attached forty-seven large rockets to his sedan chair, to which had been secured two large kites—prophesying, in effect, the wings of aeroplanes. Forty-seven coolies ignited the rockets simultaneously and Wan-Hoo vanished in a burst of fire, never to be seen again.

I was at this point in my recollections of the history of rockets in warfare when I heard on the sloping cement walk behind me a loud outcry, and turning, saw descending upon me a quite incredible missile. My first startled glance disclosed to me an impossibly fat man in a sitting posture, being propelled at me with some speed. He seemed to be waving his arms and uttering alarmed outcries. Behind him, in pursuit, was a colored man, who ran frantically, but could not overtake the adipose personage.

It seemed at first that this man was being discharged at me in a trajectory a foot or so above the sidewalk; indeed, that he was flying through the air at low altitude. But then my startled eyes descried wheels and the arms of a chair which were almost wholly concealed by the billowing bulk of the man who occupied this conveyance.

This outlandish projectile was almost upon me when I moved spryly in obedience to reflexes and removed myself from its path. Whether my subsequent immediate action was impelled by instinctive reflexes or by swiftly taken resolution, I cannot determine. Nevertheless, as fat man and wheeled chair came abreast of me, I crouched, bracing myself determinedly, and snatched. My hands closed upon the back of the vehicle, to which I clung. I found myself much in the position of the small boy at the end of the line playing the game of crack-the-whip. The chair, the fat man and I spun. Nevertheless, I clung tenaciously, with the result that, after a couple of revolutions, we came to a standstill facing in the reverse direction. Nor did the chair capsize, due doubtless to the low center of gravity and the tremendous weight of its occupant. I regained my feet, conscious of a rent in my trousers and of an abraded knee.

I stood somewhat breathless, scrutinizing the individual whom my promptness and resolution had rescued from serious injury or possible death. For a moment I doubted my eyes, feeling that perhaps my vision had been impaired by my dizzy whirl.

But I actually saw what I thought I was seeing. I saw an enormous head, a monstrous face somewhat resembling illustrations of an ogre in childhood's fairy tales. The eyes were very large and staring; under a huge and thick-lipped mouth was the great-grandfather of all chins. It was not pendulous, but solid, of the size of a considerable grapefruit. The ears were fanlike and the nose broad and flat. As to his hair, it was a repulsive shade of orange-yellow, and it stood out from his skull like an untidy halo. Never have I seen so repulsive a countenance.

The rest of the man was in keeping with his head—gross, unbelievably adipose and unwieldy. The girth of his legs and arms was fantastic and his stomach was Gargantuan. When you add to this the fact that he must have been well above average height, you have a mass of human flesh which would have aroused the cupidity and admiration of Phineas T. Barnum.

While I stared in a most unmannerly way, a voice issued from the enormous human blob. It was startling. It was quite the most winning human voice I ever had heard. It was rich, musical, beautiful. And the accents were those of a man of rare culture. It was as if the song of a mockingbird proceeded from the mouth of a hippopotamus.

"Sir," he said, "I am under no small obligation to your courage, your promptness and your agility. But for you, sir, I should now be but a gory mass under the wheels of one of those juggernauts we have ineptly named motorcars."

"I am charmed," said I, "to be of some slight service."

"Slight, sir, slight! Tremendous! Not to me alone, but to civilization. One who preserves the mind of William George Thomas from extinction deserves well of his fellow men. May I inquire your name, young sir, so that I may preserve it, not only upon the tablets of my memory but in the records which will one day be given to the world as the story of my life?"

"My name," said I, "is Thomas Alva Edison Gimp."

"Ah," said he, "there is also a name well deserving the plaudits of his fellow men." His face darkened and became angry. "Where," he demanded, "is that Ethiopian to whom I entrusted my life? Where is that beast of burden whose duty it was to propel me in this chair, using more than ordinary care to see to it that I came to no harm? I shall castigate him. Then I shall discharge him. But first I shall pelt him with hard words. I shall bombard him with parts of speech and choice epithets."

I looked about me. There was no one in sight. "He seems," said I, "to have fled."

"Well for him," said Mr. William George Thomas. "I would have burst his eardrums with such a selection of hard words as no human ear could endure. . . . But that, young sir, leaves me marooned. It is true that I can make some shift at walking, but for no considerable distance, and then reluctantly. Never could I reach the refuge of my hotel. What am I to do?"

"Why," I responded, "I fancy I can make shift to propel you to your destination."

"It is far too much to ask. Too menial a labor to require."

"Nonsense," I said briskly. "Necessity draws no such fine distinctions. Let us proceed."

He made no further protest. As we walked, he questioned me in that unforgettably musical voice.

"Young sir," he asked, "forgive an inquisitive mind for prying. What is your occupation?"

"I am," said I, "a physicist."

"Ah, a man of scientific attainments. As for me, I do not create. I do not invent. I do not produce. My vocation is to observe, to collate, to draw philosophic conclusions. I study my fellow men, their strength, their weakness, their foibles, their failures and their accomplishments. Sir, my admiration for the human species is negligible, if not to say nonexistent." He paused an instant. "Where," he asked, "do you put to use your undoubted genius?"

"My present place of research," said I, "is White Sands."

"Where," said he, "men employ themselves in devising terrible engines for their own destruction."

"We venture to hope," said I, "the destruction will be for our enemies."

"Enemies are men," said he didactically. "To destroy a man is to destroy one of yourselves. I do not mean to speak severely nor critically. You are in the mode. It is the style to invent slaughter. Perhaps you are correct. Perhaps you are solvers of the great problem."

"'What," I asked, "is the great problem?"

"To avert the disaster of an unbalanced nature where men shall reproduce themselves to a point where they bring the end of the world by the unsupportable weight of their own multitudes."

We were now in the brightly lighted area of the city. Before us loomed the bulk of a great hotel.

"This," said William George Thomas, "is my temporary habitation. If you will summon bellboys, porters, men of bone and sinew, they will relieve you of my inert bulk." His ogre face distorted itself into what I took to be a smile.

"May I hope, young sir, that your graciousness will impel you to bestow upon me the boon of your conversation at no distant day? Perhaps I shall learn how to express my gratitude by actions rather than words."

"It will be a pleasure to converse with you, Mr. Thomas," said I sincerely, for in spite of his repulsive carcass I found something about him to attract me.

I bade him good night and reached my small apartment without further interruption.

I FOUND the morning ride to White Sands not unpleasant. The bus was comfortably filled with civilian employees, among whom was Miss Brown. I was careful to take a seat at some distance from her because I did not wish my thoughts interrupted by her chatter. She waved to me as if I were a familiar acquaintance. I responded by a decorous nod.

Upon my arrival I found that the general desired me to call upon him, which I proceeded to do in his office in post headquarters. I was admitted and presented after a short wait. The general was a dignified, spare man. He received me cordially, rising and extending his hand.

"I am glad to have you with us, Doctor Gimp," he said. "Your reputation has preceded you. Have you been made comfortable?"

"Completely," I said, and waited.

"Your work, I take it," said he, "will be mainly concerned with the perfecting of the electronic brain."

"So I understand," said I.

"There are," he said with some displeasure, "skeptical people. Only last week there arrived a deputation of congressmen who seemed more interested in harrying me than in satisfying themselves of our gratifying progress."

"Indeed!" said I.

"I assured them," the general said, "that we were reaching a point where the defense of this country from invasion by air was positive through the use of guided missiles."

"I am glad to hear that, sir," I responded; however, with a feeling that he was too optimistic.

"They seemed interested," he said, "in the possibility of sending a rocket to Mars. I assured them that this was quite within the bounds of possibility. One gentleman asked if it would be possible to launch a guided missile from these proving grounds, have it circle the globe and return to the place of launching. I informed him that it would be possible; that a multiple rocket could do exactly that."

A multiple rocket is a combination of missiles, the first of which would exhaust itself and automatically be detached while the second took up the task; in turn to be dropped while the third continued on its way. Mentally I granted that theoretically this is feasible.

"Another gentleman," said he, "raised the objection that in actual warfare or in our experiments, no guided missile had traveled farther than from the launching site in Europe to a point on England. He wanted to know how we knew we could attain a more distant target."

"Have we ever," I asked, "discharged a rocket that reached a point more than two hundred miles away? Naturally, the lay mind would be disturbed."

He ignored the point. "A question was asked," said he, "as to accuracy—as to pin-pointing. I told him we could attain almost perfect accuracy if we had maps of the enemy country in which there were no errors. I explained that we could, for instance, discharge a missile from a site in America and destroy the Kremlin—if surveys and maps informed us of the exact location of the Kremlin on the earth's surface. But, I pointed out, a deviation from accuracy at the launching point of a minute fraction of an inch would result in missing the target by a considerable distance."

"True," I replied.

"But"—and he smiled—"I told them that if we could secrete in the basement of the Kremlin an electronic device that could be carried in a suitcase, the missile would search out and find that package."

"Doubtless," said I, "there would be some difficulty in penetrating the Iron Curtain with such a device under your arm and in depositing it in the Kremlin."

"Of the two types of electronic brain," he said, "I much favor the one that is wholly automatic and self-contained—which guides the missile by what we may term mechanical intelligence—over the other type, which relies for its conduct upon electrical impulses sent from the place of launching."

"And I," I agreed.

He permitted me to see his profound admiration for that device commonly called the electronic brain, which, as he pointed out, can all but think for itself, alter its mind in emergencies, give consideration to weather and other atmospheric conditions, navigate as capably as a sea captain, and, in effect, overcome unexpected obstacles and rise superior to sudden emergencies. "Unlike the human mind," he said impressively, "it is not susceptible to error."

"So we hope," said I.

"In this," said he—"in our progress toward the perfection of the electronic brain—I have reason to believe we are ahead of the rest of the world. Think of it, sir. I know that the Soviets would give millions of dollars to possess one of our electronic intelligences!"

"Doubtless," said I.

"To permit one of these miracles to fall into their hands would be equivalent to a crushing defeat on the battlefield."

"In which case," said I, "it behooves us to see to it that they do not steal one."

"Doctor Gimp," he said, "I am informed that there exists a determined effort to effect such a theft; that skillful and determined and dangerous agents have been charged with that mission. You are one who will be working upon the further improvement of this brain. You will be near it, it will be, in a sense, in your possession. Therefore I considered it imperative that I should warn you."

"I am a scientist. I work in a laboratory. It is, it seems to me, the duty of experts in the prevention of crime to protect the electronic brain and those who have it in direct charge."

"Nevertheless," said he, "you must be constantly vigilant. Doctor, it may be you whom these secret agents have chosen as the weak spot in our defenses. You will act accordingly." He arose, extended his hand again and smiled. "Good morning to you, doctor," he said.

The remainder of the day passed principally in settling myself into my new surroundings, acquainting myself with the equipment and facilities of the laboratory. I was pleased. There seemed to be nothing lacking.

AT the end of the afternoon I took the bus to El Paso. I was among the first to board the vehicle, and hoped that it would not be so crowded that I could not have a seat to myself. In this I was disappointed, for no sooner had I seated myself than someone dropped into the scat beside me. It was a woman. I did not turn my head, but presently a voice tinged with irony said, "It's all right to look now, prodigy. I'm decent." The voice was the voice of Miss Brown.

"I had hoped," said I, "to have an undisturbed trip to El Paso."

"You haven't," she said, "learned even the rudiments of what it means to be disturbed."

"Why," I asked, "do you draw that conclusion?"

"Pure logic," she answered. "Nobody—but nobody—knows what it is to be in a turmoil until I enter his life."

"You have not entered my life," I informed her.

"So? Have you ever met a poltergeist?"

"I have not done so," said I, "nor do I place credence in the existence of such psychic manifestations."

"I," she said, "am a lady poltergeist. Almost professionally. I've made a study of it."

"Why," I asked, "do you call me prodigy?"

"Why," she countered, "do you call a chimpanzee a chimpanzee? Because," she answered her own question, "it is a chimpanzee."

I did not know how to cope with such conversation.

"Do you," I asked, "understand the meaning of the term 'choke coil'?"

"A choke coil," she said promptly, "is an inductor inserted in a circuit to offer relatively large impedance to alternating current."

"Precisely," said I. "You should be equipped with one."

"You, I suppose," she retorted sweetly, "are not ignorant of the true meaning of the term 'hunting.'"

"Hunting, in electronics, is a condition of instability resulting from overcorrection by a control device, and resultant fluctuations in the quantity intended to be kept constant."

"Go to the head of the class," she said. "You suffer from overcorrection of your control devices. You're as full of control devices as a sausage is of chopped meat. What you need, Doctor Gimp, is a dose of something to eliminate your repressions."

"This bickering," said I, "is bootless."

"You started it!" she snapped. Suddenly her manner changed and her eyes concentrated upon something at a distance.

"See those mountains?" she asked.

"The Organs?" I asked.

"Right. Here we have an area forty miles by a hundred which, for security and other reasons, has been swept clean of inhabitants. Everybody inside is Army, Navy, Air Force or civilian employee of the project."

"A proper precaution," I said.

"But with an exception," she told me.

"What is this exception?"

"Two prospectors, or miners, or whatever, working in a hole up there. For some reason, they were allowed to stay."

"Doubtless a sufficient reason to those in authority."

"A raincoat," she said, "isn't waterproof if it has one tiny hole in it. So," she said, frowning, "I wonder about those prospectors."

"Leave security matters to Major Van Tuyl," I advised her.

"All the same," she said, "they bother me."

"Did you ever see them?" I asked.

"Once, on the road. They looked like two animated clumps of whiskers. Anything," she added after a pause, "can lurk in a thicket of beard."

"Doubtless," I replied, "Major Van Tuyl has combed those whiskers."

"Probably," she said unhappily. Then again her mood changed and she became rather like a little girl asking a favor of an elderly uncle. "But you will," she said unexpectedly, "take me to dinner tonight?"

I hesitated.

"If you're broke," she said, "I'll pay. But"—her voice was low, almost inaudible—"I need company tonight."

I was somehow moved. There was something about her. I had no desire to accompany her to dinner or to spend the evening in her society, but I found myself unable to refuse her plea. For it was a plea.

"Very well," said I, "if it will please you."

"I'll wear my nicest gown," she said.

"That is of no consequence," said I.

"Upon that point," she said, returning to character, "you may change your mind."

IN an hour, having shaved and put on my best blue suit, I called for Miss Brown at her apartment. A young woman opened the door to me. "I," said I, "am calling for Miss Brown."

"Present and accounted for," said she.

I stared in unmannerly surprise. My scrutiny assured me that it was indeed she, but I could scarcely credit my eyes. Miss Brown, as I knew her, had been rather a nondescript person, quite unworthy of notice. She had been not exactly dowdy, but dressed rather for work than for embellishment. Her hair was quite transformed. I had given no consideration to her physical structure, but as she stood there waiting for me to enter, I saw that it would compare favorably with that of Miss du Guesclin, though less flamboyant. I was compelled to admit that, to a man interested in such considerations, she would be exceedingly attractive.

"Don't stand there batting your eyes," she said testily.

"A quite remarkable metamorphosis," I said.

"Not," she responded, "when you have the raw material to work with."

"Even," said I, still in a state of surprise, "creditable ankles."

"And," said she, lifting her skirt a trifle, "legs to go with them. . . . Shall we go?"

"Have you a place in mind?"

"Leave it to me," she said.

Upon entering the place of her choice, I noted, and not with a feeling of dissatisfaction, that heads turned to watch her progress as we were conducted to our table.

"You arouse admiration," said I.

"Oh, that!" she said carelessly. "I'm used to it. I'm lulled to sleep with wolf whistles." As we sat down she regarded me critically and nodded. "You're not so repulsive yourself," she told me.

We gave our orders to the waiter, and while he was bringing cocktails, I glanced around the room. My eyes came to rest upon a familiar face—that of a gentleman seated on a stool at the bar.

"Ouch!" exclaimed Miss Brown in a dismayed voice.

"What is it?" I asked.

"I hope he's cold sober," she said. "The man at the bar yonder."

"Do you," I asked, "refer to Balthasar Toledo?"

"You know him?"

"I met him once," said I.

"When," she said, "he's riding the wave his dynamic stability fails to damp his oscillations."

It was a thing to stir the risibility to hear so seemingly fragile and lovely a young woman describe the vinous reactions of an individual in such terms. But I had no opportunity for remarking upon it, because Balthasar Toledo espied us and came determinedly in our direction. His extraordinarily handsome face was sullen.

"Hold your hat!" warned Miss Brown.

He walked with intention to our table and stood over it, glowering. "You refused to dine with me tonight," he said angrily.

"I was engaged," Miss Brown said. "As you can see. . . . Doctor Gimp, Mr. Toledo."

"I've met the laboratory louse," Toledo said. Apparently it was his intention to be offensive. He reached for Miss Brown's arm imperatively. "Dance," he commanded.

She did not look at me appealingly, doubtless fearing I would be inadequate to the minor emergency. I am not accustomed to such contretemps and my familiarity with social usage was not such as to guide me. I determined to rely upon instinct.

"Miss Brown," I asked, "do you wish to dance with this gentleman?"

"Decidedly not," she responded with spirit.

I looked up at Toledo mildly as he towered over us. "Miss Brown does not choose to dance with you," I informed him. "Doubtless for many reasons. The chief of which undoubtedly is your state of inebriation. The second of which could well be your atrociously barbarous manners. The third, in which I concur, could be that she does not like you. You will, therefore, withdraw."

"Keep your pedantic snout out of this, Gimp," he said challengingly, and reached again for Miss Brown's arm.

Ordinary efficiency dictated that I place myself on equal terms with him by arising to my feet. He drew back his right fist to strike me. Now, my instructors, provided by my mother, in the art of fisticuffs had informed me of the impropriety of leading with the right. It provides the opponent with a coveted opportunity. It seemed essential that I avail myself of the opportunity thus offered, which I did. I have been informed in the gymnasium that my left is quite effective. The truth of this became evident. Doubtless it was more effective than in ordinary circumstances because I was deeply offended at the man and resentful. Be that as it may, the blow landed flush and solid, and Mr. Toledo landed upon his shoulders and skidded under an adjoining table.

Miss Brown stood up, pumping her graceful arm and counting, a proceeding that I did not understand. She counted up to ten. Then she lifted my arm and announced, "The winner and new champion."

"A distasteful episode," I said in distress.

I bent over Toledo, hopeful that he had taken no serious injury. "Make him say 'uncle,' " she said softly.

I stood erect and stared down upon her. She was grinning impishly. A chord in my memory had been twanged by her words. I was taken back years, to a day when I was being chased home by a boy who bullied me, and to a little girl hanging over her fence.

"You," I said, "are the little fat girl."

"I've thinned out," she said.

"Your name was—was—" She waited while I racked my brain. "—was Melinna," I said triumphantly.

"My first name," she said, "is Melinna. It always will be. My last name is Brown. That is subject to change."

Before we could comment further upon this incredible reunion or of my recognition that it was a reunion, Mr. Toledo was reactivated. He got to his feet, not steadily, and scowled at me. He seemed now to have become sobered. His handsome face was distorted by rage, but he made no offensive movement.

"If," he said harshly, "you weren't more valuable alive than dead, I'd break your back across my knee." Whereupon he stormed away and vanished into the street.

Melinna looked up at me. She raised her brows. "To what," she asked in the tones of an inquiring reporter, "do you attribute your rapid rise in the pugilistic profession?"

"Mena sans in corpora sano," I replied succinctly.

Part Three

As I sat at my desk in the laboratory building I found myself whistling "The Star-Spangled Banner" softly. I often whistle subconsciously when engaged upon a problem. The thought came to me that the subject of rocket missiles was embedded in our national anthem in the words, "the rockets' red glare." The author of that song beheld the flight of Congreve's rockets during the British advance upon Baltimore in the War of 1812. These rockets had been of four varieties—eight, twelve, thirty-two and forty-two pounds. The thirty-two-pound rocket had a maximum range of some three thousand yards. It carried some seven pounds of shot in its conical warhead, and was stabilized by a stick fifteen feet long and an inch and a half in diameter. They were discharged from tripods, copper tubes or wooden racks, and were more frightening than destructive.

I was examining and collating certain data with respect to the flight of the big Army rocket, and to do so I referred mentally to certain elementary principles, notably Newton's third law of motion, which states, "For any action, there is an equal and opposite reaction." From this proposition all jet-engine thinking must proceed.

Now, contrary to fallacious popular belief, a jet engine does not push against the air to obtain its impetus, but is propelled by the momentum of the exhaust gasses. Hence it is possible for a missile to be sent through space beyond the atmosphere of the earth, making remotely possible a flight, say, to Mars. I was at the moment interested in the matter of thrust, which, of course, is an applied force producing motion in a body. This is not measured in horsepower, but in pounds. For instance, a rocket of the German V-2 type which travels at 3,750 miles per hour will develop fifty thousand pounds of thrust, equivalent to half a million horsepower.

I found my concentration broken. My mind insisted upon deserting the problem under consideration and disporting itself among unprofitable reflections. As, for instance, the metamorphosis in Miss Brown, the fact that she was, indeed, the fat little girl Melinna who had commanded me to fight my tormentor, and the coincidence that last night she had involved me in physical combat with the man Balthasar Toledo.

Long experience with mental processes has taught me that when the mind rebels as mine was rebelling, the most efficient method of inducing it to return to its work is either to lie prone, endeavor to clear the mind of all activity and to think of nothing whatever for a time, or to go for a brisk walk.

I determined upon the latter course. So I put on my hat and went out into the long corridor. Before I had proceeded halfway to the building's entrance guarded by a uniformed man armed with a great pistol, I encountered Miss Brown.

"I was coming to your office," she said.

"I," said I, "am going for a walk to clear my mind."

"Mine needs a spot of clearing, too," she said.

"I am walking alone," I replied.

"The mind won't behave. Is that it? Rubbish litters the path of ratiocination." She grinned at me boyishly. "I'm a first-rate rubbish clearer. . . . Wait till I get my hat."

It was useless to protest. In a moment she returned, and together we left the building.

"Ho, for the wide open spaces!" she said gaily.

I was morose. I could feel her eying me slantwise with calculation. Evidently she considered silence the course of wisdom, so we walked side by side without spoken word. We walked westward to Third Street, and then turned northward past the Naval Missile Assembly Building, on beyond the Navy Technical Laboratory, and after a time westward again into the desert itself. In the yard of the Technical Laboratory we could see piles of the torn metal from which guided missiles are fabricated. These had been recovered and brought in for study by searchers after the missiles had been discharged.

We were walking on the sand now, seeking a path amid

the greasewood and cacti and proceeding toward the distant Organ Mountains. We had walked a mile, perhaps, and Miss Brown had maintained a silence which, somehow, was companionable. She did not intrude herself, but, strangely, I found her mere presence salubrious.

We scrambled into and out of a gully and stood upon the brink of another. There we paused for breath. Idly my eyes moved about the desolation, and then suddenly were held by an object some fifty yards to our right in the arroyo. It was hidden by a growth of desert shrubs. Startlingly, a great bird, a buzzard, took flight from the spot.

"Ugh!" exclaimed Miss Brown in revulsion.

"I think," said I, "you had better stay here."

She was staring at the spot from which the foul bird had risen. "Isn't that—isn't that a human foot?" she asked tremulously.

"I will investigate," said I.

I descended into the arroyo and walked forward. As I approached, I became certain that a human foot, bare, protruded from the clump. I arrived at the spot, nor did I need to part the bushes to see, stretched upon its face, the body of a man, naked as the day he was born. It was apparent that he was dead. His face was visible in profile.

Miss Brown was at my side. She did not gasp nor cry out.

"This," said I severely, "is no sight for you. The body is naked."

"In death," she said, "there is no immodesty."

I bent over the man, fighting a squeamishness in my stomach. There was a great wound disfiguring his temple.

"Shot," said Miss Brown. "I'd guess with a rifle."

The body was that of a man past middle age, scrawny but wiry and well-muscled. Although his body was white, his face and arms were leather tanned by wind and sun.

"Odd," said Miss Brown.

"Tragic," I corrected her.

"I mean his chin and upper lip and cheeks," she said.

Undoubtedly their condition was peculiar. Although the forehead and nose and upper cheeks were the color of mahogany, the chin, the upper lip, the lower cheeks were of a much lighter shade, as if they had been protected from the burning rays of the desert sun. The man had been newly shaven!

"Obviously," said I, "he was bearded."

"Like the Bard," she said.

"It is no time to quote Shakespeare," I reproved.

"It is a time to have the screaming meemies," she said, "but I haven't them. Give me a merit mark. If Shakespeare helps, I'll quote all of *Hamlet*, with *Midsummer Night's Dream* thrown in to boot."

Something else troubled me about the face—the skin. There were two or three little slashes, as if the razor with which he had been shaved had been unskillfully applied. There was one sizable cut near the ear. It had not bled. There was no clotting.

"What is it?" Miss Brown asked, noting that I was startled.

"I believe," said I, "the man was shaved after he was dead."

"Gruesome," she whispered.

"One," said I, "would not go about the grisly business of shaving a corpse unless under strong compulsion."

"Or," she said, "stripping him of his clothes."

I noted her fortitude and firm control of her emotions with approval. "The reason for the shaving and stripping," said I, "could be to conceal his identity."

"Go to the head of the class," she responded.

"He was carried here from some remote spot."

"Maybe not so remote," she said. She started to move past the body and up the steep bank.

"No," said I, "don't scramble about. You might obliterate some telltale sign."

"Correct," she said, and became motionless.

"This," I said upon reflection, "is Major Van Tuyl's business. He should be notified forthwith."

"Somebody," she said with bent brows, "got through his patrols. But anybody could. You can't police a vast, wild area like the proving ground. All you can hope is to keep intruders from reaching the heart of it."

"Can you," I asked, "find your way back?"

"Of course."

"I will remain here," said I. "You will notify Major Van Tuyl."

"Stand on a rise," she said, "so you will be visible. Without a guide, one might search for this spot for a week."

"Right," I assured her. "Make all possible haste."

She took a final glance at me and then turned toward her destination.. It was lonesome there with nothing but the body of a murdered man for company.

Some time elapsed before a jeep came lurching over the terrain. It contained Major Van Tuyl, a sergeant and an enlisted man, with Miss Brown crowded into the back seat.

"She insisted upon coming," Van Tuyl said.

"I am not amazed," I replied.

He eyed me and I could not tell whether it was with approval or disapproval.

"Things light on you, Doctor Gimp," he said. "Things happen to you. You're a top-flight corpse finder."

"Quite fortuitously," I said.

"There are people like that. Carriers," he said tersely. "I guess maybe we made a good selection."

"Tell the major what you think," said Miss Brown.

"I think," I said to the major, "that he was shaved after death."

"Why?"

"Examine the razor cuts on his face. Some time after death."

He bent over the body and then regarded me quizzically. "A detective we got!" he said.

"A scientist you have," said I stiffly, "who observes phenomena and draws conclusions."

"Keep your highly educated shirt on," he retorted. Then he grinned. "We might have missed it," he admitted. "Do you know, with any luck this body would never have been found. In a few days there would have been nothing but bones." He pointed upward at soaring specks in the sky. "They'd have taken care of that." He walked away and in a wide circle around the spot. "Must have dropped him from the air," he said with disappointment. "No trail. Damn hard surface around here. . . . I hear you pack a pretty punch," he said.

"News travels," I said.

"Bop!" exclaimed Miss Brown, striking her left palm smartly with her right fist. "One-punch Gimp."

"You never can tell to look at them," said the major. "I had an uncle that drove screws with a hammer."

"A ridiculous thing to do," I told him.

"He liked short cuts," the major said with a shrug. "See this body?"

"Certainly."

"Maybe," he said, "it got to be a body by taking a poke at the wrong man, at the wrong time. Now you and Miss Brown better run along. You've done your good deed for the day. We'll try to handle the detecting from here. We get paid for it."

We withdrew and trudged back to the laboratory.

"Mind nicely cleared of rubbish?" she asked mischievously.

"This," I said grumpily, "was not an experience calculated to renew mental efficiency."

"What did he mean by saying you're a top-flight corpse finder?"

"I," said I, "found another one on the train. But that one had his clothes on."

"You improve as you go along," she said. "Maybe the next one will be painted blue."

"It is not," said I severely, "a joking matter."

"At the moment," she said, "I need a spot of comedy relief."

"The man Balthasar Toledo," I said, "was on the same train."

"So what?" she asked.

"So nothing," I said shortly. "It was only a fugitive recollection. He's an art expert," I added.

"He thinks," said Miss Brown, "he's a woman expert. I detest beautiful men." She stood back and regarded me solemnly. "No," she said judgmatically, "even a doting parent couldn't accuse you of that. . . . If we hustle moderately we'll be able to catch the bus to town."

We made sufficient haste and rode in together. "By the way," she said as we took our seats, "I think a combination of a knockout punch and a naked corpse put us on a first-name basis. You may call me Melinna."

THE next several days were peaceful and I was able to concentrate upon my work in office and laboratory. It was on a Thursday night that I found, upon my return to my apartment in El Paso, a note awaiting me. It was signed "Renee du Guesclin."

"Dear Doctor Gimp," it said. "It will please me if you will call upon me this evening. I shall be at home at eight o'clock."

It was brief and gave no reason for the invitation. For a time my inclination was to ignore it, but Miss du Guesclin was a woman of a variety I never had encountered before, and she aroused my curiosity. There was also the point that she was equipped with the sort of beauty which it is difficult to ignore. I recognized my desire to see her as, possibly, a weakness. Nevertheless, I surrendered to it, so that promptly at eight o'clock I rang her doorbell.

She herself admitted me, clad in a garment which I recalled vaguely was called a hostess gown. It was not a reticent gown. It emphasized rather than minimized the physical endowments of the individual who wore it.

It was, I admit, somewhat exciting. I was reminded of a woman in a motion picture to which I had once been lured—a woman who dressed in similar manner deliberately to receive company of the male sex. This I could not believe of Miss du Gucsclin, and set it down to that naiveté which, previously, I had observed to be one of her characteristics.

She extended a lovely hand and smiled up at me in a most charming manner.

"It was so nice of you to come," she said. "You think me forward to ask you, no?"

"No," I answered.

"You see," she explained, "I become lonesome talking only to the servant. One also becomes lonesome talking only to women." She smiled again, ingenuously. "It is only a man who can dispel loneliness completely."

It was pathetic that so young and lovely a woman should lack companionship and become the victim of lonesomeness. My sympathy went out to her.

We entered the comfortable parlor and, uneasily, I wondered what we would find to talk about. I have no aptitude for social conversation or, indeed, for any conversation that is not within the limits of my professional horizon. But Miss du Guesclin seemed to feel no such shortcoming. She chatted in such a manner that I presently found myself talking to her fluently and without self-consciousness.

She was graceful as a kitten. Her gestures and movements were unstudied. She seemed quite unaware of the fact that each time she stirred it served to bring to the attention some new feature of her physical perfection. There was nothing bold about it, but it served to make the beholder definitely aware that she was a desirable creature.

The conversation had been confined to trivialities. She had a bright, quick mind, but nothing so far indicated depth or superior intelligence.

"Have you," I inquired, "any compelling interest such as my own devotion to the science of electronics?"

"Oh, but yes, yes," she said quickly. "I am interested in being alive."

"That," said I, "is not a profession, nor even an avocation."

"I do not need a profession. With a profession one earns money. I do not need to earn money. Avocation—maybe I do not understand that word. But maybe it is like when one collects the postage stamp, or breeds fine horses, or becomes involved in politics. Yes? As you say, a hobby?"

"In effect," I answered.

"No. Yet I have no hobby, no avocation. But I know what it will be. Someday—I hope soon—I will have such a hobby."

"Of what nature?" I asked.

"Being in love," she said. She made the statement very naturally and seriously.

"Being in love," said I, "is not a thing one thinks about as a hobby, but rather as an emotion having its roots in biology."

"Oh, poof!" she exclaimed. "To a woman like me," she said, "being in love is a business, an avocation, a profession, a hobby. It is everything. Behol'," she said firmly, "you create a great rocket. It is to rush through the air at great speed and to explode among the enemy. That is its business. So nature create the woman for one purpose—to reach the destination and explode in love."

It was an utterly absurd comparison, repulsive alike to logic and to fact. "I have never thought of love as an explosive," I said.

"Then you do not know. Especially you do not know me. With me it will be so. Not gentle. Not the little pop of a cap pistol. But like what you call the chain reaction of the splitting of the atom."

"I fear, Miss du Guesclin," said I, "that you are fated to disappointment."

"There will be no disappointment—not for me nor for the man who has my love."

I was ill at ease. It did not seem to me that the topic of passionate attraction between the sexes was a seemly one for social chit-chat. Such discussions were better carried on seriously by sociologists or psychologists in an impersonal manner, or by a man and woman who actually stood in a relation of greater intimacy than did Miss du Guesclin and myself. But the young lady was quite uninhibited.

During my call I had occupied a comfortable sofa against the wall. Miss du Guesclin had been curled in a big chair. Now she casually stepped to an occasional table, selected a cigarette, and then, in a quite natural manner, seated herself beside me. She had anointed herself with a perfume which was far from obtrusive, but which was not without its effect upon the senses. I found that the room had become unexpectedly warm, and there was a dryness which caused me to dampen my lips. Her head rested against the upholstery of the sofa, her lower limbs were drawn up under her, and she looked up at me in a cunning manner through half-closed lids.

I had no means of knowing with certainty, but the thought came to me that she would not be resentful if I placed my arm about her shoulders. I might, indeed, have surrendered to this impulse had there not come the interruption of the ringing of the doorbell. Miss du Guesclin exhibited disgruntlement.

"Damn!" she said sharply, and for an instant her face was not that of a charming young woman with what the French term *beaute du diable* that is to say, the loveliness of inexperienced youth—but rather of a woman, capable of ruthless efficiency, furious at being thwarted in some intention.

She drew her skirt about her and walked angrily to the door, which she jerked open in temper. When she saw who stood there her shoulders twitched as though at some minor shock and she stood rigid and wordless. A soft cultured voice which I recognized at once became audible. "Miss du Guesclin, is it not?" asked Mr. William George Thomas.

"I am Miss du Guesclin."

"I should be desolated," said Mr. Thomas, "to find that I have called at an inopportune moment."

He did not hesitate for an answer, but advanced, avalanche-like, into the room, so that she retreated before his elephantine bulk. He closed the door behind him.

"My dear *mademoiselle,*" he said in his beautiful musical speaking voice, "we have mutual friends, friends who have asked me to convey to you their affection. Friends who, feeling that I might be of some slight service, have troubled themselves to send to me a letter addressed to you, bespeaking a friendly reception of myself. My name is William George Thomas."

With a manner of some grandeur he extended to her an envelope, which she took mechanically. His great, somewhat protruding eyes perceived my presence, and he bowed ponderously.

"Ah, Doctor Gimp! I have indeed intruded."

"Not at all," said I. This was true. I was relieved rather than otherwise by his arrival. It was opportune. It extricated me from a dilemma, possibly rescued me from a manifestation of my own weakness.

"May I be seated?" he said. "For obvious reasons, I find standing or walking irksome." He smiled at me. "I have secured," he said, "a more reliable propellant for my wheelchair—this time a beast of burden who will not permit me to catapult down declivities."

He lowered himself into a chair. Miss du Guesclin had opened the envelope and was reading its contents. There was a look in her eyes; there was tension in her posture.

"May I venture to hope," said Mr. Thomas, "that the note of introduction assures me a certain tentative degree of welcome?"

"It ees a note," she said, smiling mechanically, "which cannot be ignored."

I thought this a curious locution, implying rather impulsion than warmth of welcome. He regarded her blandly and then turned to mc, speaking in humorous vein, "And you, doctor, have you perfected today a rocket upon which one may ride in luxury to the moon?"

It was in the same light manner that I replied. "We have not yet," said I, "commenced to recruit beautiful stewardesses for that flight."

"Ah," said he, "a lightly tripping wit! Admirable. One does not expect the gayer *bon mot* from the brain engrossed in science. You improve, sir, you improve upon acquaintance." He clasped his enormous hands across his monstrous stomach. "Sir," he assured me, "I shall cultivate you. I shall woo your friendship. I shall sue for your delightful companionship."

Miss du Guesclin resumed her seat upon the sofa beside me, but the spell was broken. I was no longer bedazzled, nor did she seem now interested in plying me with allurements. On the contrary, she was sullen, eying Mr. Thomas with a mingling of resentment and what I took to be apprehension.

"Miss du Guesclin," said he with practiced graciousness, "you far exceed, far surpass and excel the glamorous reports that came to me of your loveliness and your charm." He beamed. "Ah, were I a younger man, as is the doctor, I would succumb with minimum struggles. Even as I am, somewhat weighted with flesh and years, I am far from impervious."

"Mr. Thomas," she said coldly, "I am not in the mood for compliments."

"And for what, dear *mademoiselle,* are you in the mood?"

"For bed," she said shortly.

She sat moodily, crumpling in her hand the note and envelope Mr. Thomas had handed her upon his arrival. She crumpled and compressed them until they were two little balls of paper enclosed in her fist.

"The dictates of decorum," said Mr. Thomas graciously, "forbid that an initial call, one purely of introduction, should be unduly extended. It matters not how strong the temptation. . . . Doctor Gimp, I find it difficult to arise from a chair without some assistance. Your hand, if you please."

The touch of his flabby hand was unpleasant, but I endured it, bracing myself as his weight caused me to exert all my strength. He stood, beaming at Miss du Guesclin and myself.

Miss du Guesclin looked up at me with eyes half closed. Her lips were compressed. There was nothing soft and yielding about her now. There were traces of, perhaps, grimness.

"You will come again soon, doctor," she said almost defiantly.

I knew that I would come again. In spite of a certain cautiousness; in spite of a subconscious warning that it might be best for me to eliminate Miss du Guesclin from my orbit, I knew that I would find it very difficult not to come again.

"Assuredly," I told her.

William George Thomas lumbered to the door and opened it. He bowed from the waist to Miss du Guesclin. He was suave, gracious, kindly.

"I regret," he said, "if my call was untimely. I blunder. I am inept."

I flatter myself that I am a shrewd judge of men. I was certain that if there was a thing which Mr. Thomas definitely was not, it was inept. I had a feeling that he had timed his call efficiently, and had a purpose. From the moment of his coming, there had been tension in the room. His manner had been courtly, but something underlay that manner, something of the cat-and-mouse variety. I was pleased that I had been able to detect it.

"Good night, Miss du Guesclin," I said. "Thank you for a charming evening."

"It was charming, wasn't it?" she asked. She seemed to accent the past tense.

"Your arm, please, doctor," said Mr. Thomas. "My equilibrium is not of the steadiest when I descend steps. It is a rare pleasure to have met you, Miss du Guesclin."

I steadied him down the steps. On the walk his wheel chair awaited us. This time it was a broad-shouldered man.

Mr. Thomas laboriously ensconced himself in the vehicle. "Do our paths coincide?" he asked.

"For a part of the way," I answered.

We proceeded a hundred feet in silence. Then he said politely, his musical voice casual, "Will you be so gracious, Doctor Gimp, as to feel in the right-hand pocket of your jacket? An odd request, eh? But I'm a man of whims. Will it astound you to find that you have a ball of paper in the pocket?"

"A ball of paper?"

"A slight thing—a thing of the size of a ping-pong ball and almost as imponderable."

I fumbled in the designated pocket and was surprised when my fingers encountered paper; not one ball, but two.

"Miss du Guesclin, doubtless in an absent-minded moment, placed in your pocket—in a moment of embarrassment, shall we say"—he smiled broadly—"my letter of introduction to the young lady."

Miss du Guesclin had surreptitiously slipped envelope and letter into my pocket. She was not one to do such a thing absent-mindedly or automatically in a moment of embarrassment. If she had concealed the balls of paper in my pocket, it had been with deliberate intention and for a purpose. For some reason Miss du Guesclin had desired me to find those balls of paper. Had I done so, curiosity would have moved me to examine them. It had been her desire that I read the note of introduction; why, I could not imagine.

"If you please," said Mr. Thomas, extending his fleshy hand.

It is a valuable thing to have a trained mind—one capable of reacting promptly to the call of emergency. Some importance must attach itself to the note. Mr. Thomas had mentioned one ball of paper when there were two. I could, of course, decline to give him what he asked for, but, ostensibly, there was no cogent reason for doing so. But one thing I could do: I could give him one ball of paper, retaining the other. The chances were even that it would be the envelope I returned to him, and not the note. I resolved to leave the matter to chance. Without exhibiting reluctance, I pulled out a ball of paper and handed it to Mr. Thomas.

He took a lighter from his pocket, ignited the paper, holding it in his fingers until it burst into flame, and then tossed it to the walk, watching it until it was consumed.

We walked together a couple of blocks, he chatting agreeably and I responding appropriately.

"I turn here," said I.

"Pleasant dreams, doctor," he said affably.

"Restful sleep to you," I rejoined.

I walked briskly to my apartment house and entered my rooms. When I had pressed the button illuminating the little parlor, I took from my pocket the second ball of paper, deeply curious to discover if chance had smiled upon me. I straightened the sheet. It was not the envelope, but the note. Upon it was brief writing, not addressed to Miss du Guesclin nor signed by any person. It contained but three words: "Stop! Look! Listen!" it said.

A command and a warning! Not a note of introduction, but an imperative and a caution. The first questions that occurred to me were these: Did William George Thomas present himself and deliver this cryptic note because I was calling upon Miss du Guesclin? Was it to interrupt that visit and to give the young lady a directive as to her behavior toward myself?

My thoughts turned to Major Van Tuyl and my initial conversation with that officer. I asked myself a third question in the terms of that conversation: Had the bleating of the kid attracted the tiger?

MAN is a mechanical object differing in certain of his attributes from any piece of machinery he himself has been able to create. The chief of these differentiations is, of course, the power to ratiocinate, to accumulate experience, which is another name for data, and to reach conclusions from his observations.

Our task at White Sands and in other centers devoted to the perfecting of guided missiles was, in effect, to endow a mechanical device with abilities so far restricted to the human brain. We had attained some success in our project to endow a jet-propelled rocket with certain of the mental abilities of a hunting dog. We had not utterly failed in our objective to install in an aerial weapon the ability to take to the air and to search out and strike an approaching and threatening enemy aeroplane. We had made gratifying strides along the road of devising an electronic quasi intelligence to be installed in a missile which was capable of meeting certain emergencies, of taking into account such matters as alteration of weather and of windage, and of correcting its navigation if outside influences deflected its true flight. We had reached a point where we knew it would be possible to frustrate and repel any air invasion of our territory if we possessed a supply of missiles adequate to that task, and definitely we would be able to launch a rocket in America which would strike in the vicinity of a target thousands of miles away.

Mr. Kipling once spoke of a dog as possessing a half soul. We have reached the success of assembling an intricate and delicate electronic half intelligence—our so-called electronic brain.

Our task, the project of employed scientists, was to bring this half brain to a further point of effectiveness when it would become a three-quarters intelligence or a nine-tenths intelligence. The duty of Major Van Tuyl and his numerous associates all over the land was to prevent the enemy from stealing the fruits of our labors.

In the motion-picture room I had been watching on the screen the preparations for the flight of a V-2. It stood perpendicular in the arch of a gantry crane while it was made ready for its take-off. The massive structure was moved away, leaving the missile standing on its tail, its nose pointing to the sky. All was in readiness. A burst of flame flattened out upon the concrete base and the great rocket seemed for an instant to stand still in the air, as if gathering its tremendous forces for titanic effort. Then, as if at word of command, the great mass of metal, held stable by the airfoils at its tail, surged upward under the impulsion of its jet motor. It vanished.

Knuckles sounded on the door and the operator of the projector opened it.

"Is Doctor Gimp here?" a voice asked.

"Here!" I called.

It was Major Van Tuyl, lean and leathery and sharp-featured, giving to the beholder an impression of wiry strength capable of sudden dynamic release.

"Fifteen minutes to spare?" he asked.

"Of course," I replied.

We walked down the corridor to my office. He closed the door. I seated myself and he sprawled in a chair.

"Characters light on you," he said, "You must have an attractive odor."

"I'm not aware," said I, "of any distinctive fragrance."

"Hackles down," said the major, grinning a bit wolfishly. "In words of one syllable, tell me about the fat man."

"'William George Thomas," I said.

"We know his name. We can estimate his weight. Deliver a brief lecture on the gentleman."

I described our meeting, the runaway wheel chair and how I had propelled him back to his hotel. I gave the facts of his intrusion during my call upon Miss du Guesclin and his presenting to her a spurious letter of introduction. I told how Mr. Thomas had seen her secrete the crumpled paper in my pocket and how the fat man had demanded its return to him.

"There were," said I, "two balls of paper. Mr. Thomas' eyes were sharp, but not all-seeing. So I selected one paper wad at random and handed it to him. He burned it and was content. When I arrived at my apartment I examined the remaining one and found that fortune had favored me. It was the note and not the envelope."

"Is the message a tender secret?" he asked.

I extracted the paper from my pocket and handed it to him.

"'Stop! Look! Listen!'" he read. And then, testily, "How long were you going to keep this on ice?"

"Until," I said, "I found time to give it to you. It may be news to you," I said ironically, "but I have work to perform."

"Yeah!" he retorted. And then, "My unworldly and pedantic pal, in this neck of the woods security comes before stratosphere."

I ignored this rebuke. "Who is William George Thomas?" I asked.

"We don't know. He just oozed out from under a damp rock. He didn't exist for us until you started capering with him." His eyes twinkled. "If he wants to keep on dancing the bunny hug with you, don't give him the cold shoulder. . . . By the way, how much hay did you make with Miss du Guesclin? I use the word 'hay' advisedly."

"Miss du Guesclin," I answered stiffly, "is a creature of sudden impulse and tenuous inhibitions."

"Some people," said he, "have all the luck."

"Have you," I asked, "identified the naked dead man?"

"Probably," he said, "someone dropped from a flying saucer. We're sending his fingerprints to the FBI on Mars. If they have one. Would you know?"

I started an informative statement upon the planet Mars, its atmosphere, temperature and weather conditions, which rendered it improbable that human life such as we know it could exist in that environment.

But he interrupted me with some discourtesy. "Tell it to Sweeney," he said. "So long, doctor. Don't worry about that attractive odor. It keeps coming in handy."

The major walked to the door, paused and turned. "Did you," he asked, "ever hear of a *femme fatale?*"

My surprise at his use of the French language must have shown on my face. He grinned. "You're not the only person who's been exposed to education."

"I never," said I, "heard the phrase *femme fatale.* What does it signify?"

"It signifies Mademoiselle Renee du Guesclin. You can have a lot of fun with one of them—if you keep your fingers crossed." He grinned again. "Renee will tend to broaden your horizon. Don't neglect her."

And then he was gone.

After lunch, I was closeted for several hours, almost to the hour of the departure of the bus for El Paso, in the exploration of a problem in terrestrial reference guidance, which is a complicated technique of missile control by which the predetermined path set into the control of a missile can be modified by a secondary device which reacts to magnetic gravitational effects which attract the rocket to its target. As, for instance, the nose of the bloodhound leads the creature to the fugitive it pursues.

I found Melinna Brown waiting among the group who were to be passengers, and when the conveyance drew up, we occupied a seat together. She seemed distrait. My own mind occupied itself with the conversation that had taken place between myself and Major Van Tuyl.

"Miss Brown—" I said.

"Why not 'Melinna'?"

"Very well, Melinna. Will you explain to me the worldly significance of the term '*femme fatale*'?"

"A *femme fatale,*" she said, turning to peer at me, "is to a man what flypaper is to a fly. It looks good, it smells good, it tastes good. But when you light on it, you're stuck."

"Ah," said I, and studied her pert face. "By any chance are you a *femme fatale?*"

"Only," said she demurely, "after office hours. I'm only a part-time one. Why? Are you in the market?"

"I merely was seeking for information."

"On that subject," she said, "you'd better confine your investigations to hearsay. You're not equipped to cope. In fact, you're not equipped to cope with a run-of-mine hussy. Nor even with a nice girl with ideas."

"Indeed!" I said huffily. No man likes to have his competence belittled.

"Doctor," she said, "you'd be a sitting duck."

"I am not," I said firmly, "so stupidly vulnerable as you believe."

"Double it," she said, "and you'd still be third-string substitute."

She held up her hand to stop me as I was about to retort. She spoke earnestly. "It's a compliment," she said. "It's the way a decent man should be. Me," she said very firmly, "I wouldn't give house room to a man who could outdicker a *femme fatale.* He'd have to be half tomcat and half snake. I'm all for men who blunder along in a straight line. They're the sort a self-respecting girl can lead to the altar before you can say Jack Robinson and apply beam-rider guidance the rest of his natural life. Which every man needs."

"Cannot a man get through life without riding a radio beam controlled by some woman?"

"No."

"A man's life," I protested, "cannot be directed by electronics."

"If they're female electronics, it can." Her eyes twinkled with mischief. "And he'll find it's just dandy."

It was puzzling. My analytical brain perceived the possibility that she was right. Because I, myself, was conscious of a need, of a lack. In the world of science I was confident of my capacity to carry on, but outside of that sphere—perhaps that narrow sphere—I was not so certain. As I looked backward I was compelled to admit that in nonscientific matters my mother had been a sort of airfoil, holding me to a certain course. I had relied upon her, permitted her to make decisions and skillfully and diplomatically to impose her wise will. Now that I considered the matter, I saw how she had dominated my father to his benefit. It could be that sex had other uses than procreation—that a man was incomplete without a woman. It was not impossible that nature had ordained that woman should be, in effect, the device by which a man's flight through the stratosphere of life should be dominated and directed. This could be a scientific truth.

"It may be," said I, "that you have stated a hitherto undiscovered law."

"Not so darn undiscovered," she said. "Eve discovered it in the Garden the day Lilith came prowling around."

"I would like to explore this theorem with you further," I said. "It presents a fruitful field of speculation."

"Well," she replied, "if you want to take me to dinner tonight, we can grub around in the fruitful field." She paused. "Sometime," she said, "the idea might pop into your head to ask me, instead of my asking you."

"It might, indeed," I answered. "In fact, it has occurred to me."

"I'll rig out in my slickest *femme fatale* costume," she said. Then she scrutinized me as if I were a specimen under a microscope. "Darned if I don't sometimes faintly suspect," she said, "that you have a nebulous sense of humor."

"Indeed?" said I. "I assure you my sense of humor is acute."

Our bus was nearing its destination. It stopped and I helped her to the sidewalk.

"In an hour and a half," she said. "It takes time for a girl to put on her *femme fatale* ensemble."

"In an hour and a half," I agreed.

I left her to step into a shop for an evening paper. When I emerged, I looked up and down the street. A block away I saw Melinna Brown, but not alone. She was walking beside a wheel chair and was in earnest conversation with William George Thomas.

Part Four

I WAS disturbed. I am not by nature a suspicious person, but events, conversations with Major Van Tuyl, and the several apparently abnormal people with whom I recently had come in contact had produced an unpleasant state of mind. I inclined to regard even casual acquaintances dubiously. Probably Major Van Tuyl would have applauded this mood. But now, suddenly, I was compelled to look askance upon one whom I had every logical reason to consider as above question.

Melinna, rising phoenixlike from the ashes of my past, had been taken for granted by me. She would not occupy the position she did at White Sands unless she had been screened exhaustively by the FBI. Her character, as I had observed it, while tending to flippancy, had impressed me as basically trustworthy. But I had seen the tragic downfall of persons occupying positions of high importance—which forced me to realize the possibility that anyone might be corrupted to the point where he became subversive or even definitely traitorous.

As I walked home my thoughts were painful, yet I strove to apply logic. By chance I had just seen Melinna Brown in serious conversation with the gross William George Thomas. Now, I had no reason to hold the fat man in suspicion, except the fact of his intrusion upon myself and Miss du Guesclin, and the cryptic warning he had delivered to her. I had no basis for believing that warning concerned myself, and certainly not just cause to suppose that it was directed against the security precautions at White Sands. It might have been personal. It might have arisen from some situation dissociated from the proving ground. Or from the secrecy necessarily surrounding our work with guided missiles.

However, it seemed to me that I was compelled to conduct myself circumspectly until the fat man's part was clarified.

IT WAS in this troubled state of mind that I called for Melinna as arranged. She greeted me with what seemed, to me, to be an innocent satisfaction with her own appearance. The satisfaction was justified.

"Do I answer the specifications?" she asked gaily.

"Specifications for what?" I inquired.

"A femme fatale," she said.

"I wish I knew," I said, not intentionally, but inadvertently, speaking a thought that had better been concealed.

She became grave, reserved, resentful. "What takes place?" she asked, her eyes intent upon my face.

I dissembled—a thing at which I have little skill. I pretended surprise at her question, shaking my head as if to clear it. "I don't understand," I said. "I fear I was distrait."

"What distraited you?" she demanded.

"I was applying Joule's constant to a certain problem with which I have been concerned. That is to say, the mechanical equivalent of heat—"

"You," she said, "are not an artful dodger." She shrugged. "Tonight let's apply the mechanical equivalent of pleasure. I crave Mexican food. How's for hopping across to Juarez? Sometimes it's gay in a dreary sort of way. I crave gay."

"To cross the border," I asked, "what formalities does one have to satisfy?"

"Practically none," she answered.

We took a cab to the customs barrier and found it was true that there were few formalities either to leaving the United States or entering the republic of Mexico. The passage of tourists evidently was encouraged. Once we had left the area of petty officials, we strolled. To me it was of interest because it was my first visit to our neighboring country. It seemed to be a town of shops purveying souvenirs and other merchandise calculated to catch the eye of the inexperienced.

"Booby traps for the bucolic," Melinna said lightly. "But if you know your way around, you can unearth real values and sometimes real bargains."

She led me hither and yon, and finally into a not too brightly lighted eating place in which was a small dancing floor and an orchestra. The main feature of this musical organization seemed to be a man who rattled things. In each hand he held a stick at the end of which was a hollow bulb containing loose dry objects. These he jiggled rhythmically. There were other instruments, notably a guitar, and a young woman with incredibly—a diamond set in one of her front teeth was singing a song in Spanish.

"The wild duck here," Melinna said, "is heavenly. And the beer. We were conducted to a table, and Melinna gave our order in the language of the country.

"You," said I, "are a linguist."

"Like the great Von Moltke," she said pertly, "I can keep silent in eight languages."

"I never," said I, "have heard you keep silent even in one."

The restaurant was comfortably filled for the most part with Americans enjoying an evening in Old Mexico. Our food arrived; it was, if not heavenly, as Melinna had described it, certainly delicious.

Soon after we had entered and seated ourselves, I saw a young man, unmistakably of the country, who came in alone and was shown to a table at our right. He was handsome, his movements were graceful—and somehow familiar. I was certain I never had seen him before, but he touched some chord in my memory. Then, suddenly, I knew whom he resembled. It was rather startling, that resemblance. He was the counterpart of that Senor Iturbe with whom I had dined on the train, and whose body I had so unpleasantly discovered subsequently.

We had finished the main part of our repast when this young gentleman arose, walked toward us and halted beside my chair. He bowed with grave courtesy. "Excuse," he said politely.

"Certainly," I responded.

"It is the Senor Gimp?" he said.

"That," said I, "is my name."

"I am Ramon Iturbe," he said. "The name, it could be, is to you familiar?"

"It is, indeed," I answered.

"May I," he asked, "intrude myself to take a seat?" He glanced at Melinna then, but not with especial interest.

I arose and motioned to a chair. "Miss Brown," I said, "may I present the Senor Iturbe?"

"Charmed," she said.

"That other one of the train," said Iturbe, "was to me the twin."

"The resemblance is remarkable," I observed.

"It ees gracious of the Senor Gimp and his so lofely companion to visit my country."

I frowned. "I take it," said I, "that your coming to this restaurant was not accidental?"

"I," he responded, "am of the *Policia Judicial Federal de los Territorios.*"

"Then this call is official," I said.

"Not so. It is personal." He paused and his brown eyes gleamed. "Someone has kill my brother. I seek that one, not official. I seek him because of the love I have for my brother."

"To take the law," I said, reprovingly, "into your own hands."

"It iss—how do you say?—an obligation of family. My brother, Juan, also serves the state. But in another part of the *Departamento de Seguridad Pithlice.* I am of the criminal investigations. He is of the branch *Policia Federal de Seguridad.* Which deal with enemies of the state, with those who are subversive."

"Your brother was returning, then, from some official errand?"

"What, I do not know. It was disclose to me that he make the journey to Washington—to speak with your FBI. It is in my mind that he return with knowledge that someone feared. With thees facts that must not reach his superiors."

Melinna sat silent and rigid. She missed no word.

"It is you, Senor, who are on that train. It is you who make the bad discovery of my brother."

"True," I answered.

"So," he said intently, "I ask you to describe thees affair."

"Senor Iturbe," I answered, "I should be glad to give you all the information I possess. But I have been forbidden to talk."

"To Juan's brother?" he asked.

"To anyone," said I.

"But," he protested, "I am of the *policia* of a friendly nation."

"But you question me," said I, "not in your official capacity, but—er—as a personal avenger."

"What would you?" he asked simply.

"I never," said I, "have had a twin brother. I do not know how I would react if he were murdered."

"Our blood is different," he said gravely. "Our obligations of family are not the same. Perhaps you of the United States leave all to the law and are content. It cannot be so with me."

"That," said I, "I am in a measure able to comprehend."

At that moment the double doors of the café were thrust wide and William George Thomas, in his wheel chair, was trundled into the room. Melinna Brown's back was toward the entrance, so she could not see the arrival.

At that instant the evening died for me. I was suddenly heartsick. To a logical mind such as mine, this could be no coincidence, but an arrangement. Melinna had brought me here and had arranged with William George Thomas to see that I would be present.

"Melinna," I said, striving to control my voice, "your friend, Mr. Thomas, has just arrived."

Iturbe shot a keen glance from me to Melinna. There was uncomfortable tension at our table.

"My friend Mr. Thomas?' Melinna asked.

"Who met you at the bus tonight," I said.

Suddenly her eyes crinkled and she grinned impishly. "I like my men well cushioned," she said.

"Are you being evasive?" I asked accusingly.

"Oh, definitely," she answered.

Iturbe was staring fixedly at the fat man. "Not," said he slowly, "a senor easily to be forgotten."

"His presence in Mexico," said I, "might be of interest to the *Policia Judicial Federal de los* Territorios."

"For what reason?" he asked.

"I haven't the remotest idea," said I, "Nevertheless, that is my opinion."

"An opinion," said Senor Iturbe, with an old-world bow, "to which a wise man should affix the attention."

Melinna continued to regard me mischievously. After her first reaction to the arrival of William George Thomas, she seemed to think the whole matter was humorous.

"Hang onto your Q-factor," she said. "It's running wild."

Perhaps my ratio of energy stored to energy dissipated was, as she thus hinted, out of balance. But I had recently been subjected to so many shocks that my normally conservative, perhaps plodding, habit of mind and action was rendered instable.

"Young lady," I said severely, "this is no moment for flippancy."

"I am not in a position to accuse you of untruth," said I, "but you will note a mental reservation."

William George Thomas gestured helplessly. "How," he demanded, "can the untutored mind of one whose avocation in life is but that of a gourmet hope to cope with the devious convolutions of the brain of an illustrious man of science? I sit befogged, bewildered, flabbergasted and in a maze."

The door of the café opened. A man stood there, a Mexican of the lower class. His black eyes roved the room and came to rest upon William George Thomas. He lifted his arm. He had a knife in his hand. There was a forward motion and instinctively I thrust at the fat man's chair with my foot. It was fortunate—for him. There was a thud, and quivering in the wooden reinforcement of the back of the wheel chair was a knife.

With incredible swiftness Senor Iturbe was on his feet, lunging toward the door. The knife thrower had vanished. Senor Iturbe, too, vanished. In the hush, the sound of running feet was audible outside.

William George Thomas moved slowly in his chair. He peered at the knife which had so narrowly missed his throat. "Ah," he said, seemingly without emotion. "Curious! Curious indeed!"

William George Thomas turned his eyes away from the knife to me.

"It would seem," he said, "that I am under an obligation to you, Doctor Gimp. It may be that I have my foibles, sir, but ingratitude is not one of them."

He signaled imperatively to his motive power. "The soil of Mexico," he said in farewell, "is not clement. I shall shake its dust from my feet. A good evening to you, doctor, and to you, Miss Brown. I trust there will be no further interruptions to your outing."

He was trundled away, massive, imperturbable. He seemed not to be shaken. Inside the repulsive bulk of him must have been nerves of iron. "From this adventure," said Melinna, "you should draw a conclusion."

"I have not yet," said I, "had time to examine its implications."

"Pounce upon the obvious," she said.

"Reason tells me," said I, "that Mr. Thomas' coming was expected and that preparations were made for his reception. One does not procure a skilled knife thrower in an instant. There was premeditation."

"Conclusion Number One," she said. "Proceed to Conclusion Number Two."

"Number Two," I said, "is not a conclusion, but a surmise: that Mr. Thomas was lured to this spot."

She nodded emphatically. "And is there a corollary to that?"

"There seems to be," said I. "It is that his coming had nothing to do with me."

"How did you scramble to that point?"

"Because," I told her, "if I had been the objective of his coming, then it must have been you who lured him. It must, then, have been you who, to use a criminal term, put him on the spot."

"Is that impossible?" she asked.

"My answer," said I, "is not based upon logic. Perhaps there is such a think as instinct. Whatever the source of my conclusion, it is firm. My reply is that it is impossible."

She smiled. "Could the source of your information," she

asked, “be the heart?”

“Nonsense!” I said firmly. “The heart is an organ concerned with the circulation of the blood.”

“Then why,” she demanded, “does it beat so furiously that it almost stifles you”—she paused and then finished lamely—”sometimes?”

“Mine does not,” I told her.

She was impish again. “Have patience,” she said. “It will.”

She had the power to create mental uneasiness. I did not wish her to perceive that I was unsure of myself.

“Shall we return to El Paso?” I asked.

“Before something else happens,” she said demurely.

I summoned the waiter and paid our check. Then we walked back to the customs and passed easily across the line into the United States. A cab was available. We were not talkative on our way to Melinna’s house. There I saw her to the door.

“Good night,” she said; “thank you for a very eccentric evening.”

“I will see you at the bus in the morning,” I said, and then was surprised at myself for saying so.

“How nice,” Melinna said, and closed the door.

I went home, undressed and retired, but sleep would not come. My thoughts darted from one thing to another erratically. I found myself visualizing the man Balthasar Toledo and his Greek-god beauty. Him I had not seen since our unfortunate encounter in the café. Melinna had not mentioned him. Then, without reason, my mind darted away to the naked body we had discovered on the desert and to the strange fact that he had been shaved after death. Something said to me almost with the distinctness of a speaking voice that he had been shaved to prevent identification. I wondered what Major Van Tuyl had accomplished in the way of discovering the man’s name. Then, and quite incomprehensibly, the two prospectors or miners who were allowed to abide in the Organ Mountains intruded themselves. I wondered what two such men, sequestered in their fastness, found to talk about. What would the attitude of two such men, shut away for months at a time from other human companionship, be toward each other? They might reach a point where they hated each other. Two unwashed, unkempt, bearded men searching for treasure, not because of the money worth of what they found, but because it was their destiny to seek, and the mere finding would be the reward.

Suddenly 1 sat erect in bed. It was the word "bearded" that had startled me. A man with a smooth face might disguise himself by wearing a beard; on the other hand, a bearded man might be disguised by removing his beard. A bearded corpse might be disguised by shaving its beard after death.

Those two men, in constant daily contact, might have irritated each other to the point of madness; little movements or peculiarities might have become hateful to a point beyond reason. One of them might have been a whistler and the other, with distempered brain, might kill to silence the whistle. So that naked corpse might not be a mystery whose solution was important to the well-being of White Sands, but only a squalid desert tragedy

It must have been at some point just subsequent to reaching this conclusion that I fell asleep.

THE alarm clock awakened me. I shaved, dressed, breakfasted and walked to the bus station. Melinna was there. This morning she was the efficient, unglamorous laboratory assistant, not the lovely, titillating woman of last night. She said good morning almost indifferently, and we occupied a seat together. "Melinna," I asked presently, "have you seen Balthasar Toledo since that night?"

"No," she answered.

"You were acquainted with him before my arrival?"

"Yes. What gives—a cross-examination?"

"He was in El Paso, then, previous to his arrival on the same train that brought me?"

"Annoyingly so," she replied. "He hasn't bothered me since that night. Maybe you left-hooked him out of my life."

We were well out in the desert when she pointed. "There," she said "is one of those prospectors."

I leaned across her to peer out of the window. We were passing an old, shabby pickup truck. On the driver's seat sat a big man with untrimmed beard, with skin burned almost to blackness, with a filthy, flopping, wide-brimmed felt hat pressed down upon his overlong greasy hair.

"Only one of them," I said. "Have you seen these prospectors often?"

"Not often," she said. "Twice or three times."

"Did you," I asked, "ever see one of them alone before?"

"Come to think of it, no," she answered. "Why?"

I shrugged and made no reply. We roared past the pickup truck and its driver, and that was that.

We alighted at headquarters, where, instead of accompanying Melinna to the laboratory, I climbed the stairs to Van Tuyl's office.

"More flies light on the sticky paper?" he asked genially.

"Last evening," I said, "was not uneventful."

"Give," he directed.

I described the events as they had occurred in the Mexican restaurant—the coming of Senor Iturbe and his conversation with Melinna and me. Then I related the more melodramatic incident of the attempt to kill William George Thomas by knife thrower. But I could not bring myself to relate how Melinna had met William George Thomas upon the arrival of our bus in El Paso, nor how she had walked away with him in earnest conversation.

"But," said I, "it was not last night's excitements that I came to relate."

"I suppose," he said ironically, "you thought them scientifically negligible."

This I ignored. "I came primarily," said I, "to state to you a conjecture."

"Which is?"

"That the nude body we discovered was that of one of the prospectors you have permitted to ply their vocation in the Organ Mountains."

"Based upon what?"

"Beard," said I. "Shaven beard."

"Oho!" exclaimed Major Van Tuyl. "You mean, doctor, that his killing might not have been a matter affecting security at all, but merely the result of a quarrel between partners?"

"That," said I, "would be reassuring."

"It would," he answered. "Run along now and have a happy day playing with your electronics. I'll put the microscope on prospectors." He eyed me in a humorous manner and shook his head. I walked out striving to control the irritation he awakened in me.

DOCTOR Newcomb was awaiting me with certain data derived from the discharge and flight of a Viking rocket which had reached an altitude approaching the F-1 layer of the ionosphere some one hundred and twenty-five miles above the earth's surface.

"It has been said," he observed, "that the speed of a rocket is limited to the speed of light."

I nodded. My mind was proceeding along another line. "We must always bear in mind," said I, "that the rocket is the only jet engine capable of operating outside the atmosphere—that is, in interstellar space—because it is the only jet engine carrying its own oxidizer. Rocket propellants consist of an oxidizer and a hydrocarbon fuel. The oxidizer, of course, is liquid oxygen, nitric acid or hydrogen peroxide. The fuel may be gasoline, alcohol, liquid hydrogen, aniline."

"Elementary, my dear Doctor Watson," he said smilingly.

"Our particular concern," said I, thinking aloud, "is guidance-control systems. There must be included in such a system attitude control and path control. Suppose we discharge a missile without attitude control. It may decide to tumble end over end or roll. A missile cannot be guided unless its attitude to its path of flight is controlled so that it will always point in the desired direction without oscillation or roll. But in addition to attitude control, it must have path control, to insure that its flight continues in the direction of the target. But we are seeking something beyond these things. We are seeking to perfect an electronic intelligence which will report and correct all errors; which will seek out and contact its target, whether in motion or stationary. In flight the rocket must be able to navigate as a ship captain navigates; it must smell out and track its target as a bloodhound tracks a fugitive. To be completely effective, this intelligence must be contained within the rocket and not supplied by outside impulses. In other words, the perfect guided missile must become an independent mechanism. That perfection we have not attained."

"But nearly," said Doctor Newcomb. "We have accomplished so much that Soviet Russia would consider it a rare bargain if it could purchase that device"—he touched with his foot a container not larger than a good-sized suitcase—"and transport it across the ocean to its own electronic scientists."

"The brain," said I, looking down almost with awe at the small device upon which so much of scientific labor and solid treasure had been expended.

"You or I," he said grimly, "could become a millionaire if we could contrive to smuggle that container and its contents out of White Sands and deliver it to enemy hands."

"Has such an offer," I asked, "ever been made to you?"

"No," he said grimly. "They don't work that way. They're more adroit."

I continued to stare at the container, which I could lift without severe strain. "If," said I, "I succumbed to temptation and managed to get this thing past the security guards, I wouldn't know what to do with it—to whom to deliver it." I smiled loftily. "One couldn't," said I, "stand in the market place and shout that one was offering for sale to the highest bidder an electronic brain."

"Doctor Gimp," said he, "do you suppose that every man in a position such as yours and mine has not been screened as carefully by Soviet intelligence as we were screened by the FBI before we were trusted to carry on our work? I'll venture that there's a dossier on you and me in some Soviet filing cabinet so exhaustive and exact as to astonish. The enemy will know our every weakness, our every ambition. He will know what temptation is most apt to destroy our loyalty. He will have looked for sins upon which to base blackmail."

"Not pleasant to contemplate," said I.

"It also," said he, "is not pleasant to contemplate the fact that these miscreants will be seeking a way to entangle you in some unsavory mess which will place you in their power. Or, if they cannot do that, to—as the underworld expresses it—frame you. These people will stop at nothing. Men like you and me live under a constant threat."

I never had heard Doctor Newcomb talk in this manner. It alarmed me. I never had thought of myself as an individual of interest to a foreign power. I never had considered the possibility that I might become enmeshed in some web capable of destroying me. I felt suddenly as if an invisible hand were pointing a weapon at my heart.

"So," said Doctor Newcomb gravely, "keep a weather eye peeled. Walk the straight and narrow. Suspect your dearest friend. Suspect me." He paused impressively. "I had a dear friend," he said, "who shot himself. The reason could only be guessed at. My suspicion is that he was faced with the choice of betraying his country or being charged with some turpitude which would have stripped him of all he held dear. He chose not to betray his country."

We dropped that unpleasant subject and returned to study of the data that lay before us on the desk.

It was just before five o'clock that my telephone rang. It was Major Van Tuyl.

"Doctor," he said irritably, "you gave me a tough day's work. Stick to science and don't go hunting mare's nests. I went into the Organs to the prospect hole of those two prospectors. They were both there. They were both alive and profane, complete with whiskers."

"I'm sorry, major," I said.

"Don't be. It was good reasoning."

A thought occurred to me. "Major," I asked, "are you certain they were the same two miners?"

There was a prolonged silence. Then he spoke testily. "Doc," he said, "you've got the most annoying type of mind I ever bumped into."

"It has been called a rather superior intelligence," I said stiffly.

"It could be, at that, Doc. But it's a darn nuisance." With that, he hung up abruptly.

IT WAS on the following Thursday evening that I found a note awaiting me on my return to my apartment. It was from Renee du Guesclin and was rather urgent in nature. It was almost in the nature of a command.

"You have been neglecting me," it said. "You will come tonight at seven or I will know that you do not wish to be my friend. We will dine here together, and then we shall see."

It was both a threat and a promise—a threat that if I did not accede to her request, there would be nothing more; and a promise, not definitely expressed, that the evening would not be uneventful. I stood holding the note in my hand and studying my reactions to it. One of the most beautiful women I ever had seen was, to put it baldly, making advances.

Any man with pretensions to masculinity would be stirred. I was complimented. That so lovely a person should favor me as she seemed to do was flattering.

I gave myself a word of caution. I asked myself if there could be any underlying motive to her invitation which might be dangerous to me. I admitted that possibility. At the same time I took into consideration the urging of Major Van Tuyl that I expose myself to advances that might be made. From this reflection it was easy to convince myself that, even if risk was involved, it was my duty to accede to Miss du Guesclin's demand.

Consequently, I dressed myself with care, and, at seven o'clock, presented myself at Miss du Guesclin's door. The impact of her appearance was powerful. She was even more lovely than I had pictured her. She seemed younger, more appealingly helpless and naive. And her greeting was such as to arouse in me a sensation of acute pleasure. She extended both hands in welcome and drew me into the house.

"I was afraid," she said, "that you would not come."

"Why should I not come?" I asked.

"You might," she answered, "have misconstrued the coming of that dreadful fat man."

"My training," I said, "is not to reach conclusions except upon adequate demonstration." I countered with a question, "'Why did you put his note to you in my pocket?"

"Because," she said, sitting close beside me on the divan, "I was frightened."

"Of what?"

"Of that monstrous man," she said, and pressed more closely against me.

"Why?" I asked.

"I don't know. I never saw him before, but he terrified me. He is an evil man. He reeked with evil. Could you not sense it? An emanation! And that message!"

"It was a warning and a command," said I. "What did it signify to you?"

"Nothing," she answered, "It meant nothing. 'Stop! Look! Listen!' Is of the railroads, is it not?"

Her lovely hand with its tapering fingers reached for mine and clutched it. This was not unpleasant. It was not unpleasant, even though the most rudimentary intelligence would detect that she was lying. The message had a meaning to her, a meaning well understood.

She shivered. "I am cold," she said, "not cold as in winter, but cold with fear. Put your arm around me."

She was indeed trembling. Fear was upon her, and it was a genuine fear, not simulated. But as I placed my arm about her shoulders she did not feel cold. She was alluringly warm. I was inclined to think more about her and her proximity than about the puzzle she presented. I was conscious of breathing more heavily than is my custom. A question occurred to me: Was she aware of the emotion she aroused in me or was her conduct instinctive, the actions of a frightened young woman seeking reassurance?

"Miss du Guesclin," I asked firmly, "are you for some reason trying to seduce me?"

She did not withdraw from me nor did she seem offended. She did, however, lift her head and smile at me.

"It is the gentleman," she said, "who seduces the lady."

"I doubt it," I answered.

"But it must be so."

"I disagree," I replied. "It is the lady who supplies the allurement. She makes herself desirable; she employs devices to make herself more beautiful; she exerts wiles to make the gentleman desire her. By these methods she disturbs him and brings him to the point of making overt advances. If these advances are successful, he cannot be accused of seduction. No charge can be made against him except that his powers of resistance have been overcome by adroit strategy."

"And your powers of resistance?" she asked.

"At the moment," said I, "I find them unstable."

"You are a funny man," she said. "You make love as if you were in a laboratory."

"I am not making love," I said firmly.

"Then what do you do?" she asked, and laughed a tinkling little laugh that was derisive. "You sit beside me. Your arm holds me. My head is on your shoulder. What you call that, eh?"

At this interesting moment a bell rang outside the door. Miss du Guesclin sat erect.

"It is dinner. You and I, we shall dine. Afterward, then we shall argue again if you make love. Eh? We shall settle that point."

It was a simple but excellently prepared dinner, served by a girl who might have been Mexican or Indian. During the eating of it, Renee du Guesclin and I did not approach either the subject we had been discussing or that of William George Thomas and his cryptic note. The girl came in, bringing dessert, and Miss du Guesclin said to her, "After you have cleared the table and washed the dishes, you may go to your home."

Undoubtedly that had been the understanding with the servant when she had been hired for the occasion, and equally evidently, Miss du Guesclin took this means of making it clear to me that presently we would be alone in the house.

We returned to the living room, but not to the divan. Not that I was reluctant, but I wanted to keep my head clear at least for a time. And then, unexpectedly, I found myself thinking about Melinna Brown. This was disconcerting. I was able clearly to visualize the expression that would settle on Melinna's face if she should see me on that divan, my arm around the seductive Miss du Guesclin and her head upon my shoulder. The thought of that expression caused me to squirm. Not that it was any of Melinna's business.

I coined an aphorism: No man can cope with more than one woman at a time. To which I added, dubiously, a corollary: And quite probably not with one.

Miss du Guesclin peered at me slantwise, with invitation in her eyes.

She patted the divan beside her.

"Come to me," she said.

"Presently," I replied. "I want to consider."

"Is this," she asked, "a time for consideration?"

"I wish," said I, "to look before I leap."

"Look at me, then," she said, leaning toward me, "and then, it may be, you will not have the hesitation to leap."

She frowned as the telephone rang. To me, this was welcome relief from the necessity to make a decision. I listened.

"Yes, thees is Miss due Guesclin. . . . No, it is not convenient. . . .It is not convenient because already I have a caller. . . . Good-by."

She replaced the receiver and turned to me. I could see that her eyes were troubled. "It was a business," she said. "I do not wish to be trouble with business tonight."

"When I was here before," said I, "your telephone rang."

"True."

"And afterward William George Thomas intruded."

"That is so."

"Do you imagine he or someone else will intrude tonight?"

"Because of the telephone call?"

"Yes."

With bent brows, she stood peering at me. "Of me," she said, either sadly or with spurious sadness, "you are suspicious."

"Let us say that I have a mental reservation."

"But why—why?" she asked, and came nearer to me.

"Because," said I, not guarding my words, "the bleating of the kid attracts the tiger."

Her eyes grew big. "But that means nothing. It ees not an answer. What ees thees kid—this small boy, is it not? What ees this tiger?" Her English became more foreign.

"The kid," said I, "is not a small boy; it is a baby goat. It is tied to a stake, where it bleats in the darkness to lure the tiger to the hunters."

She thought about that and shook her head as if she did not understand. "It is a figure of speech," she said. "Am I this baby goat?"

"No," I replied.

"Am I, then, thees tiger?" She paused. "Or am I thees hunter?" She shrugged her alluring shoulders. "Thees is so stupid," she said. "Me, I am no leetle goat. I am no tiger. I am no hunter. I like better to be hunted—to be hunted by you. Let us, then, forget thees things of the jungle, and be just man and woman in thees nice room."

I heard the closing of the back door. The servant was gone and we were alone in the house.

"Now," she said, "we shall be as we were."

She did not sit again on the divan, but moved to the door of her room. "In a moment I will return," she said. "For a moment you will be patient."

She closed the door behind her. I sat and considered if the better part of wisdom was not quietly to withdraw while she was gone. That would be discourteous, but it would be final. I got to my feet and stood hesitant. Then I sat down again. I might have vague suspicions of Miss du Guesclin, but no certainty. She might indeed be what she wished me to think her: merely an exquisite girl of hot Latin blood, who had, without rhyme or reason, become infatuated with me. That was not impossible. Women have become infatuated with less likely men than I.

If this were not the fact—if, on the contrary, she were using her beauty to accomplish some purpose perilous to me—that very thing might be what Major Van Tuyl desired. He had promised that I would be watched and guarded. I am not certain which consideration was the one that induced me to remain—Major Van Tuyl or the promise of Miss du Guesclin's luscious beauty and desirability. At any rate I did not carry out my half-formed intention to take my departure.

Miss du Guesclin did not return promptly. Five minutes passed and her door did not open. I wondered what complicated cosmetics she might be using to enhance unnecessarily her loveliness. I admit to a measure of excitation.

Ten minutes passed and I became definitely impatient. Fifteen minutes passed and I became uneasy. I remembered the brief telephone conversation. This added to my uneasiness, and uneasiness became alarm.

Nothing normal could cause Miss du Gueselin to remain absent so long—not when her eyes had shown such eagerness to return. It might be that she had fallen suddenly ill; that she had fainted.

It got to my feet and approached her bedroom door. I hesitated, and then rapped. There was no response. I turned the knob reluctantly. I opened the door.

Miss du Gueselin lay upon her bed, one exquisite limb exposed. She was very still. I walked to the bed. The top of her dainty hostess gown was wet and stained with red. I bent over her and lifted her hand and felt for the pulse beat. I could find none. I ventured to place my hand over her heart. There was not a throb.

I knew a moment of stark terror. While I had sat a few feet away, someone had entered her room, stealthily, silently, and stabbed her to death. Almost within reach of my hand this monstrous thing had been done, and I had been helpless to prevent it.

In the first moment of shock I did not consider my own position—that I was here, alone with the body of this beautiful dead girl. But then awareness of my predicament came to me.

Murder had been done, and I was there with the victim: There could be no other result than that suspicion should rest heavily upon me—hard suspicion, if not certainty. Motive would not be wanting—the age-old motive of sex. I could see myself under arrest, on trial, sentenced to punishment by a stern judge. I could see the ruin, if not the termination of my life itself. I stood appalled.

I stood there for minutes. I grew somewhat calmer. I forced my eyes to look again at the mortal remains of Renee du Guesclin.

It was then that I saw a folded paper beside her outflung hand. My first thought was that here was hope; that here was a suicide's note which would save me.

I snatched it, read it—read its incredible message. The message was directed to me, printed crudely.

"Doctor Gimp," it said, "the lady was expendable."

Part Five

IT SEEMED an interminable time before I recovered from the initial shock of finding Renee du Guesclin's murdered body. But it could have been only a matter of moments before my mind resumed its functions and I became aware of the plight in which I found myself.

It was evident that I had been adroitly selected to be the scapegoat. Action rather than thought was indicated. The impulse to self-preservation asserted itself.

My duty as a citizen demanded that I notify the police and await their corning. But to do so would be, it seemed to me, to surrender to the planning of those who had brought me to this pass.

I picked up the paper upon which was the message. It had been penned by a hand hardened to the taking of human life—by a ruthless, cynical, evil hand. I lifted it and put it in my pocket.

Then, acting swiftly but efficiently, I removed from the house such evidence of my presence as might be there. With my handkerchief I wiped possible fingerprints from the knob of the dead girl's bedroom door. I repeated this precaution, wiping every object my fingers could have touched. For an instant I scrutinized the room to see if there remained any indications of my presence. And then I took my departure through the back door, from the back door into an alley, and walked by a roundabout way to my apartment.

The point of danger was the girl who had cooked and served the dinner. Undoubtedly the police would find and question her. Or it might be that, with the fear of the police inherent in her class, she might remain mute and invisible. It was possible that all the information she could give the police was that some man, nameless to her, had dined with Miss du Guesclin. It was a thing I could do nothing about. To ignore it was my only course.

As I walked I had time to consider. I reasoned with trained efficiency. I asked myself what the perpetrators of this deed could gain by my arrest and conviction for murder. The answer was they would gain nothing. If this was the case, why had it been planned that I should be placed in such a position? The solution of that problem was not far to seek. Someone possessed knowledge. That knowledge would be held over my head for purposes of blackmail. Not the sort of blackmail that demands cash payment, but the sort that demands some action in return for silence. And that action could refer to nothing save the position of trust I held in the laboratory at White Sands. Murder, I was convinced, was to be used as an instrument to compel me to betray that trust.

I felt some resentment against Major Van Tuyl and the FBI. He had assured me that an eye would be kept upon me, a protective eye. On the other hand, in all fairness, they could not be expected to supervise every engagement I kept with a lady. I could not hope they would supervise my every moment. Certainly they had no way of knowing that I would leave my apartment that night and go to Miss du Guesclin's house. I could not accuse them of being remiss.

I had been in my apartment less than fifteen minutes when my telephone rang. I lifted the receiver from its cradle and said hello.

"Doctor Gimp?" asked a voice.

"Speaking," said I.

"Are you sure," the voice answered, and its tone was unpleasantly jocular, "that you removed all your fingerprints?"

"Who are you?" I asked.

"That," said the voice, "is for you to worry about. You can wipe away fingerprints, but you can't wipe away eyewitnesses."

"Come to the point," I said.

"In good time," he replied. "There's also the matter of the girl who served your dinner. Ignorant little thing. But if you were to be stood under a bright light, she'd be sure to identify you."

"Again I suggest that you come to the point."

"We just want you to know where you stand," he said. He laughed shortly. "It's a nasty feeling not to know when a policeman's hand will clap you on the shoulder."

"A worry," said I, "that you might be sharing with me."

"The man has spirit!" he said admiringly. "You won't enjoy stewing in your juice. Tougher lads than you have broken under it."

"You have not yet," I said, "arrived at the point."

"The point is," he said, "that we may have a slight favor to ask of you. Not at the moment. But when the time comes, we hope you'll be in a state of mind to grant it. Good night, Doctor Gimp. Sweet dreams."

The line was dead. I replaced the instrument. They had been prompt to let me know where I stood. It was upon an unpleasant spot.

I doubted that I would be able to sleep, but eventually I did so.

MY alarm clock awakened me. I dressed, breakfasted and made my way to the bus stop. I would have preferred not to find Melinna Brown there, but she was waiting with the others, and I could not avoid her. She bade me a cheerful good morning, to which I responded shortly.

"Grumpy," she said. I grunted in response.

"Wrong side of the bed," she said, and shrugged. "It's important data."

"What," I demanded, "are you talking about?"

"A girl," she said, "should know about it. How a man wakes up. The statistics aren't to hand, but two will get you five that more homes are busted up at breakfast than at any other time of the day."

"You're talking nonsense," I said.

"No, indeed! But, on the other hand, I'd loathe a man who got up singing madrigals. Whooping around the house."

"And I," said I, "don't care for a young woman who goes whooping around in a bus."

"I didn't whoop," she said. "I merely burbled." She eyed me mischievously. "What happened last night to put you in a foul humor this morning? Wouldn't the lady play?"

"How," I asked unguardedly, "did you know I was with a lady?"

"I didn't," she said. "But I do now. Would it be that alley cat masquerading as a Persian kitten?"

"How," I demanded, "do you know about her?"

"You recognize the description," she said tartly. "Oh, I have my spies around." She crinkled her eyes. "You'd better stay another year in the minors. You're not ready for the big league yet." Her eyes were not altogether friendly now. "You'd be a sucker for the hidden-ball trick."

"Your language," I rebuked, "is crude."

"Friend of my childhood," she said, "you don't know the rudiments of crude. Wait till you see me swap words for actions. I'll show you a set of crude that'll curl your inhibited hair."

"Will you desist," I said, "from chattering? I wish to think."

"I will," she told me, "if you'll say 'uncle.' "

That word took me back through the years to the little fat girl swinging on the gate. Suddenly my resentment against her impertinence subsided and another emotion took its place. There was no resemblance between Melinna Brown's slender loveliness and that rotund child who had shamed me into belligerence so long ago—not physically. But inwardly, imponderably, she was that same little girl—the child who had first aroused in me an interest in rocket ships as she read from a paperbacked book in the shade of a lilac bush. That little chit had done something to me and for me. She had come briefly into my life and then disappeared from it. But she had modified me and suddenly I felt welling up in me a surge of gratitude to her.

"Uncle," I said in a voice that made her turn her head and peer at me. Her strait look became a gamin grin.

"Well," she said, "I'll be damned!"

"If," I asked her presently, "you were in a quandary—a serious quandary—what would you do?"

"That would depend," she answered.

"Upon what?"

"Upon," she said, "whether my quandary affected myself alone or if it had to do with others. It would depend upon whether right and wrong were mixed up in it. It would depend upon whether my decision involved courage or cowardice. I think, if it was a bad quandary, I would take it outdoors and expose it to the mountains."

"What do you mean by that?" I asked.

"You can't rub elbows with the majesty of great mountains and be small or mean or cowardly. They advise you. 'My strength cometh from the hills,' " she said gravely.

I sat silent. I peered from the window of the speeding bus across sunlit reaches of the desert toward the rampart of mountains, and corrected her quotation, "I lift mine eyes unto the hills from which cometh my strength."

"I guess," she said softly, "you've answered your own question." I had done so.

The bus stopped at the administration building. I climbed its broad steps and ascended to the second floor, where I walked to the office of Major Van Tuyl, chief of intelligence and security. I did not have to wait, but was shown at once into his private room. He looked up from his desk and his eyes were saturnine.

"What caper now?" he asked.

"I," said I, "am putting myself in your hands."

"My hands are pretty full," he said sourly. "But maybe I can crowd you in. Give."

"Nobody," said I, "is agreeable to being accused, tried and convicted of murder."

He leaned forward and fixed me with level, shrewd eyes.

"Who," he asked, "has been murdered?"

"A woman," I answered, "named Renee du Guesclin."

He inhaled a sudden breath. "When?" he asked.

"Last night," said I, "between nine-thirty and ten."

"How," he asked, "do you get fingered for it?"

"I was there," I said. "I found her body."

"That makes three," he snapped. "It's a habit." He paused an instant.

"How did you stumble over this one?"

"I didn't stumble. I was there."

"In her house?"

"Yes." I tossed across to him her imperative note of invitation. He glanced at it, frowning.

"Somebody slipped," he said.

"I went. The lady was in a seductive mood. I will not say I would not have responded. She was desirable."

"Luscious," he said.

"There was a cryptic telephone conversation." I repeated to him what I had heard. "She served an excellent dinner. Afterward her conduct was no less seductive. She went into her bedroom, leaving me alone. I waited. After fifteen minutes, I became disturbed. I rapped on her door, but there was no response. I walked in. She was dead."

"And then?" he asked.

"I picked up the message."

"What message?"

That, too, I passed to him. He read it aloud, "'Doctor Gimp: The lady was expendable.' "

He grunted. "And then?"

"I wiped away my fingerprints as best I could. I removed evidence of my presence, and went away from there, using the back door."

"Anything else?" he was terse.

I repeated, word for word, the telephone conversation which had taken place after my return to my apartment. And then I was angry.

"You asked me—directed me, in fact—to let myself be used by you and the FBI as a lure. I acceded to your demand. But I didn't foresee that it would result in the murder of a beautiful girl. I would have been no party to such a thing."

He, too, became angry. "Do you think I or the FBI deals in murder? Do you think we would procure a murder or permit a murder to be done, for any purpose?"

"You are a ruthless lot," I said.

"When the security of our country is threatened, we can be

ruthless," he answered.

"The lady was expendable," I said.

"Not by us."

"And I suppose," said I, "that I am expendable too."

"Any one of us," he answered, "is expendable if the situation requires it." His face became less stern; he smiled grimly. "You are expendable, Doctor Gimp. But we shan't squander you. We're not that prodigal."

"Reassuring," said I ironically.

"You didn't actually slip a shiv into this du Guesclin woman in a moment of overenthusiasm?" he asked.

"What do you think?" I asked stiffly.

"I think," he said, "that you're too valuable as bait to be expended. Just yet."

"Will you have to disclose everything to the police?"

"Not the El Paso police nor the state police. We're fishing for sharks. We can't have our bait gobbled by flounders."

"So," I asked, "what do I do?"

" 'They also serve who only stand and wait,' " he quoted. "Just sit still, doctor, and see what lights on you next."

"And meantime," I said sourly, "I shall have the same efficient protection as last night?"

"We can't sleep with you," he said shortly. And then, "They made no definite demand upon you?"

"No. I was to stew in my juice."

"That means they're not ready. Their plans, whatever they are, are not complete."

"Plans," said I, "to steal the electronic brain?"

"What else?" he demanded. "Now scram," he said, and as I reached the door, "We'll try to do a better job of chaperoning from now on."

"I hope so," I said dubiously.

I walked to the laboratory. I found Doctor Newcomb awaiting me in some impatience. He wanted me to go with him to the Army building to which the wreckage of a Nike had been returned the night before by the searching crew. It was a crumpled mass of metal, but we were hopeful that enough remained of its electronic equipment for us to study and from which to draw conclusions.

The space at the right of the building resembled a junk yard. It was littered with the remnants of rockets which had been discharged in the past. Of some of these, little remained which could be of use.

In order to preserve as much of the recording equipment as possible, the bigger rockets had a mechanism which detached the head containing the recording devices after the rocket attained a certain altitude, the theory being that a smaller and less streamlined portion of the rocket would fall with less velocity and be subject to less destruction than if the mass of the rocket plunged to earth as a whole. This was not true of the needlelike Nike, whose movements were recorded by radar, by recording stations along the road of flight and by the miraculous devices contained in that building beyond the launching sites. The roof of that flat structure bristled with radar dishes. There was mounted a repaired and improved monster, taken as part of the spoils of the invasion of Germany upon which the observer could sit in his seat and observe the flight of the swiftest missile. Inside the structure itself were a multitude of mysterious, miraculous devices for recording upon lined sheets of paper by moving arm and stylus every movement, every deviation, every gyration of a missile in flight. It was a building housing such incredible accomplishments that it might well have been named the House of Miracles.

After we completed our observations we lunched at the officers' club. It was a hot day. We were in need of some relaxation, so we were driven to the Navy's swimming pool over beyond the NCO club to refresh ourselves by a dip in the cool water.

As we emerged from the dressing room, clad in bathing suits, we saw a small figure poised on the highest platform of the diving tower. She stood a moment, arms outspread, and then her body plunged downward in a graceful, skillfully executed movement known as the swan dive. She emerged from the water a dozen feet from us, and for an instant created the impression of nudity. But there was a scant bathing suit, nevertheless, and inside the bathing suit was Melinna Brown.

I stared. I admit it without shame. I stared. Never in my limited experience had I seen a body so exquisitely formed. No engineer on his drawing board could have drawn a mechanism of such perfection of line—a perfection eloquent of efficiency to perform the various functions required of a human body. But I ceased to think of Melinna Brown in scientific terms. I found myself thinking of her as a woman, and it would be only a slight exaggeration to say that I was enraptured by what I saw to draw conclusions.

She became conscious of my scrutiny and grinned at me impishly. "Like it?" she asked, and then ran toward the shelter of the dressing rooms.

I emerged from a somewhat dazed condition to find Doctor Newcomb regarding me with a quizzical expression.

"She does affect people that way," he said dryly.

MY telephone rang and it was not necessary for the caller to identify himself by name. I recognized the voice, that musical, cultured voice of William George Thomas.

"Doctor Gimp," he said, "I have been remiss. I am under obligation to you which I never can repay, but which should have been acknowledged ere this. My excuse is that I have been indisposed."

"I am aware of no obligation," I answered.

"Nevertheless," said he, "I shall be gratified if you will dine with me this evening at my hotel. If you will so far gratify me. At eight o'clock, if that is not too late. May I expect you?"

I doubted that the fat man was one to be overly concerned about an obligation, if one existed. That he had some covert purpose in offering me hospitality seemed more likely. The only way I could learn what this might be was to accept his invitation. I was unable to see how any harm could come to me in the dining room of a reputable hotel. There was also the likelihood that the FBI would be more alert than on the tragic evening when I had dined with Miss du Guesclin. I resolved that they should be alerted.

"I shall be agreeable to dining with you, Mr. Thomas," I said to him.

"I'm delighted," he answered. "At eight o'clock, then."

Immediately he was off the wire I called the field office of the FBI. "This is Doctor Thomas Alva Edison Gimp," I said when I was connected to the special agent in charge. "I have just accepted an invitation to dine with William George Thomas at eight in the dining room of his hotel."

"Thank you for notifying us, Doctor Gimp," was the reply.

I did not think it essential to dress for the occasion, but I did don a freshly pressed suit. I was prompt. I entered the dining room exactly at eight. Mr. Thomas already was there, seated in his wheel chair at the table he had reserved. His bow of welcome, though he did not arise, was stately and the smile that lighted his repulsively flabby face was warm.

"It is more agreeable," he said, "to be alive than to be dead. Unless you be one of those who believe the hereafter to be a time of eternal delight. I, myself, prefer to prolong the more ponderable enjoyments available to a body of flesh and blood, rather than those of a more tenuous and undemonstrated nature promised to a disembodied soul. I thank you for enabling me to do so."

"It was but a muscular reflex," I answered. "I saw the knife. Quite mechanically I kicked your chair."

"Then," he said, and there was sincerity in his musical voice, "I shall transfer my gratitude to your co-ordination." He peered at me a moment. "One would not have expected such instantaneous muscular response to sudden stimulus from one who lives not in a world of action, but in one of the intellect."

"My mother," said I, "was insistent that the training of the body should parallel the training of the mind."

"Well for me that she did so," he said graciously.

He had ordered the dinner with the skill of a gourmet and we addressed ourselves to the consumption of it.

"Superb food," said he, "deserves undivided attention."

With this I agreed. It was not until we had eaten our fill that any significant word was spoken. Then it was uttered with a rueful humor.

"Doctor," he said, and his slits of eyes above the fat of his cheeks twinkled with good humor, "you fooled me rather gorgeously some nights ago."

"In what manner?" I asked.

"In the matter of the note I delivered to Miss du Guesclin, which she secreted in your pocket. The late Miss du Guesclin. Her tragic and untimely end, her inexplicable taking off, is puzzling our local constabulary. The joke was on me. I congratulate you upon your adroitness. But, may one ask, to what end?"

"I am of inquiring mind," said I. "Otherwise I would not have chosen the field of research as my life's work. I noted various phenomena which aroused my curiosity."

"Naturally," he said easily. "And what theory did you form?"

"I am not one," said I, "to postulate a theory upon insufficient data."

"Excellent," he said cheerfully. "In certain scientific explorations it is axiomatic that the collection of data is not unaccompanied by peril to the collector. There might be detonations. There might result poison gases, or infections, or those unhappy results which come from the handling of such elements as radium."

"Any chemist," said I, "is aware of the chances he takes."

"The reactions of human beings," he continued, "may be more astonishing than those of chemicals."

"Of that I am also aware. Would it not be better if we gave over verbal fencing, Mr. Thomas? Did you invite me here this evening to promulgate a warning or to pronounce a threat?"

"I would not be so crude, Doctor Gimp. I was but indulging in dialectics. I was playing with an idea, frolicking with cause and effect."

Before I could make reply to this evasion, the man Balthasar Toledo entered the dining room, brushed aside the headwaiter and strode between diners to our table. One could not but admire the Grecian perfection of his face, its classic proportions, the broad brow, the lack of indentation above the nose. Since

I had seen him, there was a difference, but it was a difference of coloration. His skin was a chocolate brown, tanned by wind and sun, and his wrists and hands had taken on the same coloration. Mr. Toledo had been exposing himself to the climate of the region.

He did not wait for an invitation, nor did he trouble himself with courteous greetings. On the contrary, uninvited, he drew a chair from a neighboring table and seated himself between us.

"So," he said harshly to Mr. Thomas, "you came out of your burrow."

"One must needs come up for air," said Mr. Thomas. He chose to be amused. "Even you and I," he said, "must observe the amenities. You are, I believe, acquainted with Doctor Gimp. You have not greeted him."

The look Balthasar Toledo turned upon me was not friendly. "I have met Doctor Gimp," he said shortly.

"So it has been reported to me," Mr. Thomas said with meaning.

"It was," said I, "rather an encounter than a meeting."

"Which I have not forgotten," Toledo said. "You have been dodging me, my fat friend," he said to Thomas.

"Not dodging. My build—as you so amiably point out—is not adapted for the agility involved in dodging."

"The time has come," said Toledo, "when you and I must talk."

"About what, my friend?"

"Do you want me to tell you with this pedantic nuisance listening?" Mr. Thomas waited as if hoping for me to make some reply. I thought it essential that I should do so.

"Mr. Toledo," I said, "I am not one easily to take offense, but I find your manner repulsive. Indeed, I find a great deal about you to be repulsive. I hope you will see fit to mend your manners."

"And if I don't?" he demanded belligerently.

"Why, then," said I, "I shall feel it incumbent upon me to give you a second, and perhaps more emphatic, lesson in decorum."

He made as if to push back his chair. His face was dark, his lips drawn back viciously. Before he could make a belligerent movement, Mr. Thomas spoke. His voice was not gracious now, nor musical. It snapped like a whip.

"Sit still, Toledo," he said. And then, less imperatively, but softly ironical, "Is your business such as needs advertisement??'

"Send the—" Toledo paused and amended his speech. "Ask Doctor Gimp to excuse himself. The time has come for you and me to talk."

"Doctor Gimp is my honored guest. You are an intruder. Why should we discuss, Toledo? Our interests are inimical."

"Matters have reached a point," Toledo said, "where we should join forces."

"An admission of weakness, my dear Toledo. I am conscious of no such necessity. I find myself adequate, quite competent to carry to success the project upon which I am embarked."

"Half a loaf," Toledo snarled, "is better than no bread."

I looked across the room. At a table some dozen feet away, against the wall, sat a young man in a neat blue suit who might have been an attorney at law. He was eating slowly, engrossed in his dinner. But somehow, as I noted his presence, I was reassured. I was chaperoned.

The more or less cryptic conversation between Thomas and Toledo was interrupted. As it had proceeded I was not unhappy to discover that they were at cross purposes. Now they fell silent as a fourth person, showing beautifully white teeth in a smile, came to our table.

"Good evening, gentlemen," he said. "Ees it permitted that I shall join you?"

It was young Senor Iturbe, brother of the man who had been murdered on the Golden State Limited. I remembered my manners even if Toledo had forgotten his. He was there. I performed the introduction.

"Senor Iturbe," said I "this person is Mr. Toledo. Mr. Toledo, Mr. Iturbe is a member of the *Policia judicial Federal de los Territories* of our sister republic of Mexico."

"Charmed," said Senor Iturbe.

Toledo contented himself with a curt inclination of the head.

"But I am here for the pleasure," said Senor Iturbe. "As you come to my country for the pleasure so soon ago. Not official, no. Oh, very personal." He turned to me with a genial smile. "You have not shoot off another great, disobedient rocket which come bang into our graveyard. That ees nice. Our dead people do not like to be disturb' before the day when all must awake."

"I'm sure," I said, "our missiles will be better behaved in future." I spoke to no one in particular, but let the remark drop casually. "Senor Iturbe," said I, "is brother to that other Senor Iturbe who met his death on the Golden State. You, too, were aboard that train, Mr. Toledo."

"I and a hundred other people," he said.

"He," said I, "was not expendable." I scrutinized the faces of Toledo and Thomas as I said this. There was nothing to observe, no change of expression, no sudden start.

"My brother," said Iturbe, "might have been expendable to my government. But not to me. I have been grant' a—how do you say?—leave of absence. Yes. To attend to family affairs. It is a family affair to show to someone that a brother is ver' not expendable."

He smiled from one to the other of us as if he had been talking about something light and inconsiderable, but somehow it was more impressive than if he had uttered savage threats of vengeance. There was a brief silence. Then Toledo bent over the table toward William George Thomas.

"Will you talk with me later tonight?" he asked.

"No," said Thomas succinctly. It was the first time I ever knew him to be brief. Usually one had to mine his meaning out of a gush of words.

"In the morning?" Toledo urged.

"Not in the morning. Not in the afternoon. Not at any time in the future, my friend. To urge a conference upon me is a confession of weakness, of uncertainty. You, my good competitor, have been abysmally stupid. I am averse to associating myself with crass stupidity. A very good evening to you, sir."

Toledo surged to his feet. There was the pallor of rage beneath his coat of tan.

"You'll be sending to me," he said between his teeth, "and I promise to kick your messenger in the teeth." He turned vindictive eyes upon me, but did not speak. Then he shrugged his magnificent shoulders and strode away.

"Thees gentleman," said Iturbe softly, "is of a disposition not agreeable."

William George Thomas smiled a baby's smile. "He is a gentleman of culture, a critic of the art of painting whose judgment is sought. The shoemaker should stick to his last. There are, my friends, varying degrees of adroitness. There is that perfect finesse which stands at the head of the list. In it is no emotion, but only cold intellect. The lowest form of all is animal cunning, which, in emergency, may confuse brain with muscle and resort to violence. Our friend Toledo possesses a modicum of animal cunning. It has sufficed to gain for him a reputation in certain quarters."

He turned his pig eyes upon me. "But, my young friend, he is not to be underrated. Especially when he is very stupid he must be considered with care. I recommend caution to you, Doctor Gimp."

"Should I also be wary of you, Mr. Thomas?"

He was not offended. "You are thinking of the note to Miss du Guesclin which you so adroitly prevented me from recovering." He nodded to Senor Iturbe. "Sometime," he said with amusement, "I shall tell you how neatly Doctor Gimp outwitted me.... No, doctor, you need not be wary of me in the sense that you should be wary of our friend Toledo."

"Yet Miss du Guesclin is dead," I said.

"Is it not possible," he asked, "that, had she read and heeded the words of that note, she might still be alive to ply her interesting avocation? But we are rude. We talk of matters of no interest to my other honored guest."

"I listened," Senor Iturbe said.

"Did you," I asked, changing the subject to one more calculated to be of interest to our Mexican friend, "apprehend the man who threw the knife?"

"Oh, yes," he said easily. "Almost at once. He is a not nice person who will throw knives at anyone for a few pesos."

"I think," said Mr. Thomas, "that it would be the part of wisdom for me to eschew a town where that service can be hired so cheaply." He smiled broadly. "I do not present a difficult mark." He stirred in his wheel chair. "We have dined excellently; we have enjoyed both good and dubious companionship. It has been a complete evening. Nothing can be added to that which is complete."

"And I," I agreed, "must rise early."

"Then shall we say, till we meet again?"

We moved to the door of the dining room, I propelling William George Thomas' chair. There we said good night. As I left the hotel I was not displeased to note that the young man in the neat blue suit was sauntering along behind me.

The research for which I had been sent to White Sands concerned only indirectly the operation of a jet-propelled engine, but rather with the complicated electronic devices by which a missile propelled by such an engine could be controlled and directed in flight. It was necessary, of course, to understand the working of a jet engine. Now, contrary to popular belief, a jet engine does not obtain its forward motion by pushing against the air. It does not squirt out a stream of gas against anything. Hence, it can operate in a vacuum, in rarefied upper air or in interstellar space in which there would be nothing against which to push. It makes use of the principle set forth in Newton's third law of motion, which states, "For any action there is an equal and opposite reaction." That is to say that, for example, when you discharge a gun, sending a bullet out of the muzzle, there is a backward kick against the shoulder. It is upon this principle that the jet engine is based. Therefore, there is present the rather romantic possibility of constructing a rocket that could travel through space to some other planet.

The problems upon which I was working had little to do with the problem of propelling a missile to such tremendous distances, but rather with navigating that missile so that it would, for example, reach the planet Mars instead of Saturn. Or, in less magniloquent terms, to reach Moscow instead of missing that target by fifty miles.

Numerous minds in the field of electronics had produced this brain. Our task was further to improve that brain or to perfect it. Its nature, component parts, its *modus operandi,* was the most jealously guarded secret of White Sands. Its secrets were coveted by an inimical foreign power. We knew that Russia would expend any treasure or toss away any number of human lives to wrest it from us.

Major Van Tuyl was convinced, as I, myself, was alarmingly certain, that the various melodramatic events in which I had been concerned were all parts of a plan, skillfully conceived and adroitly carried forward, to abstract an electronic brain and to place it in the hands of Moscow.

"More and more," he said to me grimly, "it emerges that you are elected to be the goat."

"An unenviable position to occupy," said I.

"The sweet spot in the whole mess," he said, "is that they have no idea you know you're the patsy. I hope—for your sake."

"Why for my sake, major?"

"Because," he said, "so long as they keep on believing you're a sap-headed scientist who isn't hep to the facts of life, you're too valuable to damage." He grinned in a manner that I considered wolfish. "But," he went on, "the minute they discover that you're being used as a lump of sugar for their flies to light on"—he made an unpleasantly suggestive gesture, drawing his finger across his throat—"I wouldn't write insurance on you for a thin dime."

"That," I said, "seems to give you gruesome satisfaction."

"Not so, doc. I'm impressing you. Yeah. The more firmly you can convince them you're a guileless nincompoop the longer we'll have you with us. Not," he said half under his breath, "that you'll have to be a magnificent actor."

"I may," said I severely, "be a nincompoop and guileless, but I haven't shied away from accepting the risks involved.'

"Hell, doc," he said, not at all apologetically, "Van Tuyl's fourth law of intestinal fortitude says that even a nincompoop can be a hero, if the wind's in the right direction."

"I'm not a hero," I said testily.

He shrugged. "I wouldn't know," he said. "Most heroes I've known were young fools who had good luck in the pinch."

"Except the dead ones," I observed.

"You got a point," he said.

I walked to the laboratory. Presently Melinna Brown came into my office and perched on a corner of my desk.

"All research and no monkeyshines," she said, "make Thomas Alva a dull boy."

"In the laboratory," said I, "a trifle more respect is indicated."

"This," she retorted, "is an interlude."

"For what purpose?" I asked.

"The day after tomorrow is Sunday," she said.

"Of that I am aware."

"Six of us," she said, "are going for a sort of picnic over in the Organ Mountains. There will be Commander Pettingill and his wife, Mr. Knowlton and Miss Wilkins and me."

"'That is five," said 1.

"And you," she said with an impertinent grin.

"No," I said promptly.

"Yes," she said with equal promptness. "I suggest that you stay here over Saturday night. We will make an early start Sunday morning. We will meddle with flora and fauna, to say nothing of beefsteaks."

"But I—" I commenced somewhat weakly.

"I knew you'd be delighted," she said, and hopped off my desk.

When she was gone, I considered the matter and found the idea not unattractive. Indeed, a day in the open might prove a welcome break in my routine, which was confining. A diversion of this kind, in the company of Melinna Brown, might be enjoyable. I found myself anticipating it with some pleasure.

So it was that I slept in White Sands on Saturday night after dining in the officers' club with Melinna and accompanying her to an absurd motion picture in which criminals and a detective shot weapons at each other endlessly and an idiotic young woman was rescued from a predicament in which a moron could not have entangled herself.

IN THE morning early, dressed suitably for such an outing, we drove out of the town on the Las Cruces road, which, after crossing the desert, climbed rather windingly and steeply over the mountains to the little city twenty-six miles away.

We were crowded in the car which Melinna had somehow obtained from the car pool. The women wore shirts and blue-jean trousers, and Miss Brown, at least, made an attractive picture. After an ascent we found a suitable spot for parking, and the commander, who seemed familiar with the terrain, led us back from the road and down into a small canyon floored with sand which was to be our headquarters for the day. We amused ourselves by constructing a crude fireplace in which to broil our steaks and in stretching a square of canvas as protection against the sun.

These chores completed, Melinna Brown said to me in rather a pointed manner, "Let's you and I go and scramble."

"Don't get lost," said the commander's wife amiably. "Don't break a leg, and look out for rattlers."

I would have preferred to remain sedentary, but Melinna was disturbingly energetic. "And besides," she said, "I want to lure you off into the solitudes where I can do a job of work on you. If I find I'm in the mood."

We set off down the canyon, and after a time Melinna manifested a desire to climb. It was indeed a scramble. We reached the top of a low ridge. Before us the mountains arose grim and forbidding. The prospect was one of inclement rocks, of sparse vegetation—an arid, jumbled wasteland. Melinna was set upon exercise and seemed tireless. I knew it would be useless to protest. She did, at last, consent to sit down upon a flat rock, and I stretched at her feet.

"You're panting," she said. "You're out of condition."

"I am not," I said, "a mountain goat."

"Wouldn't it," she asked, "be comical if we got lost and all White Sands had to turn out and comb the mountains for us?"

"It would," I said severely, "be humiliating."

She seemed very young and childish in her rough attire. Even her face did not seem to be that of a mature woman, but of an elfin little girl—rather a naughty, mischievous brat. She bewildered me. At one time she would be the completely competent and sexless laboratory assistant; at another time she would be an alluring woman of the world, meticulously groomed and sophisticated; at another time, as now, she would be completely *gamine.* It was not easy to keep abreast of her moods or of her several outward appearances.

"Well," she said, her eyes crinkled, "here we are a thousand miles from anywhere. Aren't you going to make a pass?"

It chanced that I was familiar with this bit of argot. I was shocked. "You," said I severely, "don't know what you're saying."

"Why do you think I lugged you away off here at the hills?"

"I am amazed," I said.

"Well, aren't you?" she demanded.

"I certainly," said I, "am not going to make a pass."

"How very uncomplimentary!" she exclaimed. "After all the trouble I've been to—and skinning my knees!"

"Miss Brown!" I said severely, my intention being to speak seriously to her of the impropriety of her words. But she interrupted me.

"I just wanted to find out," she said. "I mean, if you harbor a quart or two of red corpuscles. Up to and including now, you haven't even tried to hold my hand. Let alone kiss me good night. So I just positively have to find out if you're equipped with jet propulsion or if they left out a combustion chamber when they built you." She jerked her head up and down three or four times. "I know some men need a launching device before they can get up speed. I thought that might be it. But you don't seem to launch."

"My respect for you, Miss Brown—" I began formally, when she interrupted again.

"Oh, hell's bells!" she said in a hopeless tone. "Listen to instruction. Maybe you can't assimilate it, but here are a few basic facts: Just because a man makes a pass doesn't mean he'll get anywhere. Point Number Two: if a man fails to make a pass, a girl gets the idea something is wrong about her. Point Three: if a man neglects to make a pass, a girl knows there's something wrong with him."

I was firm. "Definitely I have no intention of taking advantage of you in circumstances—"

"Give ear, friend. When anybody takes advantage of me, it's after I've made full arrangements to be taken advantage of. I deduce that you're hopeless. This has been a piece of necessary research. I guess I've found the answer. You're not a missile at all. You're just a dummy model—for exhibition purposes. . . Let's go scramble some more."

She sprang to her feet, and I followed, feeling that somehow I had proved myself inadequate. I had failed to rise to the occasion. But she had misjudged me. It was not that I lacked a propellant or an oxidizing agent, nor that I required a launching device. The point which she missed altogether was that it was not inertness that restrained me, or even so-called moral considerations. The real point was that, when the time came for me to make a pass or other demonstration of admiration and affection, I would make it under my own power and not as the result of any provocative overtures on the part of the female. For that I would select my own place, time and method.

I could assume from the carriage of her shoulders that she was disgruntled. She marched forward with chin in the air, but it did not add materially when she stumbled over a stone and would have fallen on her nose had I not caught and supported her. She shook off my hand testily. She was not heading back toward the place where we had erected the fireplace, but was trudging morosely farther back into the mountains. I knew she would manifest stubbornness should I make a suggestion, so I remained mute.

For some time we proceeded in an unsocial manner. Then she paused, lifting her nose to sniff. She looked at me with an inquiring little gesture, exactly as if there had been no unpleasantness between us. Her mood had changed again with inexplicable swiftness.

"I smell smoke," she said.

"Maybe our friends have started the fire," I said.

"The wind's in the wrong direction. It's ahead somewhere,"

I frowned. "Who else would be building a fire in these mountains? Could it be one of Major Van Tuyl's patrols?"

"I think," she said gravely, "that the research department should research."

"That's Van Tuyl's business," I told her. "If it's someone who has no right to be here, they might become unpleasant."

"Afraid?" she asked.

"Yes," I answered.

"Always a good idea," she smiled. "It makes for caution."

I stood sniffing. There was a distinct aroma of wood smoke. The slight breeze was carrying it to our noses down the ravine upon whose floor we walked.

"We're Injuns," she said, delighted with her idea. "We slink."

We proceeded, treading cautiously. The ravine veered sharply to the left. It ceased to be a ravine and became a canyon with perpendicular, towering walls, a box canyon. As noiselessly as we could contrive, we approached its gateway, concealing ourselves among huge boulders. There was a slight rise in the ground up which we climbed. From its top we could look down into the narrow box canyon, and there, not a hundred feet away, was a wood fire and the aroma of coffee and bacon. Beside the fire, squatting on their heels, were two men in the crude habiliments of prospectors. They were bearded, unkempt. Standing against a rock were two rifles.

Melinna put her lips close to my ear. "The old prospectors," she said. She was about to disclose herself, but I gripped her arm and drew her back.

Sounds carried in that constricted space. We could hear

distinctly the little noises of their movements as they poured coffee into tin cups and removed sizzling bacon from the pan. They ate without speaking to each other, while we watched hungrily.

Melinna looked at me with a little questioning smile. She saw no reason why we should not disclose ourselves to a couple of weatherbeaten prospectors whose presence inside the limits of the proving grounds had been sanctioned by authority. But somehow I was not at ease. Unbidden, the recollection came to me of the dead man with the shaven face that I had discovered yonder on the desert. It was true that some of Major Van Tuyl's men had investigated and reported that it could not be one of the prospectors because both of them were visible in their usual haunts. Nevertheless, I heard a tocsin ring a warning.

My suspicions were quickened when the taller of the two men reared to his feet and extracted a cigarette case from his trousers pocket. The sun gleamed on silver. The man lighted a cigarette and a pungent odor came downwind. It was a Turkish cigarette.

It would have been unnatural for an old prospector to smoke a cigarette, unless it were one he rolled himself. One would have taken a pipe for granted. But a Turkish cigarette! And a silver easel. That was too much.

There was nothing about the other, smaller man to cause me to think him spurious. He was the first to speak, and then not in the Western vernacular which one would have expected. His accent was thick, guttural, foreign. It did not seem to me to be German. In spite of his pronunciation, he struck me as being an educated man; his English was fluent, his sentences correctly formed. It was only that the words were spoken by an alien tongue.

"You assure me," he said, "that id vill be nod many days."

"I can't tell how many. We can't hurry things."

"True. Ve must nod be careless now. But id is nod comfortable in these mountains."

"You'll be able to be comfortable all the rest of your life," answered the taller man. "'We'll turn the thumbscrews this week."

Melinna's fingers dug into my arm. I looked sidewise at her. Her cheeks were pale, her lips parted, her eyes seemed inclined to start from her head.

"The fat one," said the smaller of the two. "I fear him more than all these security guards, than the FBI."

"He will be taken care of."

"You failed in Juarez."

"Putrid luck," answered the taller man.

"Take care he does not have better luck than you. That pachyderm! Once, in Spain, he balked me. Once, in Iraq, he all but had me murdered. That one is not to be laughed away."

The taller man shrugged. "Confound this underbrush," he said. "On a hot day like this it is unbearable."

His hands went to his tangled beard. With a little effort that thicket of whiskers came away from his chin and left his face exposed. They would have deceived anyone, no matter how keen his eyes. A work of art. This disguise had been fashioned and applied by a skilled hand.

Again Melinna's fingers dug into my arm painfully. An exclamation of astonishment almost was wrung from my own lips. For the face that was disclosed in that bright noonday sun was the face of a Greek god. The features were those of Balthasar Toledo.

Part Six

"PUT that thing on again," the guttural man said sharply. "If you are careless when there is no danger, there may come a time when you are not cautious with danger present. Act always as if spying eyes were upon you."

Toledo snarled a reply. He fitted on his beard again and the guttural man helped and scrutinized until he was satisfied it had become again a perfect work of art.

"Never again," the man went on. "When a part is played, never for an instant abandon that role. It is not efficient." He paused and frowned at Toledo. "Even you," he said grimly, "are expendable."

"You threaten me!" said Toledo.

"I caution," said the guttural man. "So now you return to El 'Paso, openly. The more often you are seen, the more they become used to you. Now we will go."

They gathered the several articles of their equipment, shouldered their rifles and passed within fifty feet of where we crouched. I was afraid the sound of my breathing might reach their ears. A slight movement, the overturning of a pebble, might betray us and I was not so fatuous as to think, if we should be discovered, that we should ever reach White Sands again.

But they trudged away unconscious of our presence. I maintained a firm grip upon Melinna's arm and we crouched there in silence for so long a time that I was assured it would be safe to move. Even then I was determined upon caution. I did not stand erect, but peered about me over the rim of the rock that sheltered us, to make sure Toledo and his companion had in actuality gone away. And then I compelled Melinna to remain hidden while I crept away from the box canyon and peered down the ravine in the direction they had taken.

Having assured myself so far as was possible, I returned to Melinna. "Walk softly," I said. I quoted the words of the guttural man: " 'If you are careless when there is no danger—' " I said.

"Toledo!" she said.

"Precisely."

"But he—he made passes at me," she muttered.

"You might have been useful to him," I told her.

"No," she said. "Not that altogether. He—he fell for me. That was real. He was jealous. He was troublesome." She seemed appalled. "I've been made love to by a murderer."

"You mean the real prospectors?"

"Of course," she said shortly. And then, "I want a bath."

"That nude body we found. The corpse shaved after death. One of the prospectors," I said.

"So," Melinna said, "they could establish an advance post within arm's reach of 'White Sands."

We were picking our way with what rapidity we could manage toward the rendezvous with the remainder of our party.

"No word to them, if you please," I warned her. "This is for Major Van Tuyl."

"Of course," she assented.

It was a relief to rejoin our friends, and it was a relief to them to have us appear. They had felt anxiety. The midday meal had been delayed for our benefit, and we sat about the fire eating with good appetite.

I was no longer in a holiday mood, and even Melinna was subdued. My desire was to get back to headquarters and consult with Major Van Tuyl, but it would be difficult to break up the party without creating a situation and informing our friends that something of an untoward nature had happened. Therefore we amused ourselves in various juvenile ways until the afternoon waned.

It was approaching dusk when we arrived again in the town. We dropped off our companions at our quarters, turned our automobile back to the car pool and walked to headquarters. It was our good fortune that Major Van Tuyl had been detained in his office by paper work, and he received us with no outward manifestations of pleasure.

"Well, doc?" he said. "What now? Every time you show up it's trouble. Whose body have you found this time?"

"A pair," I said, "of very live bodies."

He turned saturnine eyes upon Melinna. "Where does she fit into this?" he demanded.

"She's another body finder."

"You're wondering," she said, "if Doctor Gimp has been indiscreet."

"I could be wondering just that," Van Tuyl said.

"When he was made," Melinna said in a disgusted tone, "indiscreet was left out of his cosmos."

"Was it left out of yours?" His eyes were hard as they bored into hers. "I've been meaning to ask you," he said. "What's your tie-up with William George Thomas?"

She darted an accusing glance at me. I felt myself flushing. One does not relish being caught at tale-bearing.

"The accused stood mute," she answered.

"I can jerk you up as a security risk," he threatened.

"You'd better jerk up some of your own men as blind or incompetent," she said tartly. It was a characteristic feminine maneuver of answering an inconvenient question with an irrelevant accusation. "They don't look under whiskers."

"Under whose whiskers?" he asked.

"Prospectors' whiskers," she said, and it was evident she had diverted him. "After we found that shaved corpse," she said, "you sent some of your people to see if he was one of our two miners back in the Organs."

"Yes. They reported both men O.K."

"But they didn't test the whiskers—say by giving them a good hard tug."

"No."

"They'd have been surprised," she said.

Major Van Tuyl turned sharply to me. "What's she talking about?" he snapped.

"I will be more explicit," I said. "We went on a picnic today. Miss Brown suggested that we wander off alone."

"For a definite purpose," she said unpleasantly.

I ignored this interruption. "We scrambled some distance

into the mountains. The odor of smoke became noticeable. It aroused our curiosity. In a box canyon we saw two bearded men cooking over a fire."

"We scrooched down among the rocks," Melinna interrupted again.

"Presently," I continued, "one of them found his beard uncomfortable and removed it."

"What?" demanded Van Tuyl loudly.

"It was no Santa Claus beard," Melinna said. "It was a dandy. You'd never have suspected it."

"The face underneath," I said, "was that of a man named Balthasar Toledo. The other man, who seemed to be his superior, reprimanded him. This other man was a foreigner—an educated foreigner. I took him to be Slav."

Van Tuyl waited for me to continue. "Toledo," I said, "was about to return to El Paso." I paused here and glanced at Melinna. "They were," said I, "apprehensive of William George Thomas. The guttural man, in effect, ordered Toledo to remove him."

"As they tried to do in Juarez," Melinna said.

"It seemed," said I, "a matter that should be reported to you."

"So now," Melinna said, "you can go and pick them up."

"No," I said emphatically.

Van Tuyl fixed me with very shrewd eyes. "Why not pick them up?" he asked.

"On what charge?" I asked.

"Murder," said Melinna.

"Or threat to security," added Major Van Tuyl.

"No," I repeated.

"Who gives orders here?" Van Tuyl demanded.

"You do," I said, "but I hope they will be wise orders. Why," I asked, "have Toledo and the Slav established themselves inside the proving ground?"

"To spy," said Van Tuyl.

"Nonsense," I answered sharply.

"All right, Mr. Mental Prodigy, why?"

"As a receiving station," I answered. "A handy receiving station for stolen goods. One that would not be suspected. One from which a couple of investigated old prospectors would be able to remove the stolen goods to a destination. Mexico is indicated."

"What stolen goods?" asked Van Tuyl.

"The only thing," I said, "that would justify so elaborate a plot. The one thing above everything else in White Sands that the enemy covets. The electronic brain."

"So," asked Van Tuyl, "what wise orders should I issue?"

"None," said I, "that would betray your knowledge. None that could warn the plotters, whoever they may be. You can arrest Toledo and his companion. What do you accomplish? Conviction of murder, possibly. Or of illegal presence within the proving ground." I shook my head. "They would only turn to other devices, send other agents. It would seem to me," I continued, "that your objective should be to smash the plot and apprehend all, not a couple, of the plotters."

"Major," said Melinna pertly, "the doctor is quite a figure-outer!"

"You start," said I, "with this advantage. If the brain should be stolen, you know where it will be taken. Enabling you to take correct precautions."

"Just how," he asked with some sarcasm, "do you think these people can get at the electronic brain, our most carefully guarded secret? How do you think they could sneak it through our cordon of security? You can't carry a can of sardines past our guards without accounting for it."

"I think it could be done," I said.

"Maybe the Russians better retain you for the job," he snorted.

"I conceive," said I, "that I have been selected for that chore."

"Now, doctor!" Major Van Tuyl said, as if speaking indulgently to a child.

"I am convinced of it," I said emphatically.

"No!" exclaimed Melinna Brown. "No. No."

"Examine all the facts known to you, Major Van Tuyl. You will—probably you already have—reached the same conclusion."

"Continue," he said icily.

"A situation might arise," said I, "in which it would be efficient for you to permit me to abstract the brain."

He smiled thinly. "Do you, perhaps, realize that any such action on your part would come close to treason?"

"I have considered that," I answered.

"That you might be accused of being a traitor to your country?"

"That danger," I said, "is inherent."

"You would take that risk?"

It was an unhappy moment, but it had to be met. "It seems," said I, "to be an emergency in which even a man's good name could be expendable."

"You advise?" he asked shortly.

"That you do nothing to put them on their guard."

"I shall have to confer. I shall have to consult my superiors and the FBI."

"Naturally," I answered.

"And if they agree to this waiting game?"

"In that case," I told him, "it seems to me the best procedure is to continue to let the bleating of the kid attract the tiger."

"I read Kipling," said Melinna. She was regarding me in a disturbing manner, rather wide-eyed, with a sort of breathless intentness.

"Doc," said Van Tuyl, "you're either a fool or quite a warrior."

Melinna's eyes were dark and deep with some emotion which I could not define. She reached out her arm and touched my hand lightly. "Major Van Tuyl," she said rather formally, "my theory is that he is a little of both."

"Miss Brown," he said with even greater formality, "you have, through circumstances, been permitted to listen to matters that you should not have heard. Do you realize that I could order you to be taken into protective custody where you couldn't talk?"

She looked at him with level eyes. "Do you think that is necessary?" she asked.

He returned her gaze, and then his thin lips contorted themselves in a smile. "Somehow," he said, "I think it will be unnecessary. Now scram! Both of you! I've got to talk to sane and important people. No more time for a pair of screwballs. Scram!"

I had spent the evening with a member of our scientific staff and his pleasant wife. The time had passed quickly—not, possibly, for my hostess—in a discussion of homing systems. Certain complexities are involved which could offer little of interest to the ordinary female mind. Certainly it was not social chitchat. We had commenced our discussions with a definition of homing systems and a fixation of terms to be employed. Namely, that a homing system in a guided missile is a control device inside the missile itself by means of which the direction of the rocket can be altered in flight to pursue its target. There must be, of course, a seeker in the missile corresponding in a sense to the sensitive nose of a hunting dog. This must keep the missile automatically pointed at its target, even though the target be in motion. It is some characteristic in the target which feeds information to the computer to keep it informed of the target's location and guides it to a direct hit.

Characteristics of the target which may be observed and made use of by the seeker are emissions of light or of radio, radar reflectivity, infrared emanations, sound, capacitive features or magnetic properties. We discussed the relative merits of active, passive and semiactive homing systems with respect to their efficiency in defending against an attack by enemy airplanes or missiles, and at various points the discussion became almost heated. I, myself, contended in favor of a system employing the constant-bearing principle—namely, that the missile proceeds on such a course as to intercept the target at a predicted position, its advantage being that its accuracy increases as it nears the target, and its disadvantages that its range is limited and that special launching devices are required. My friend voted in favor of the combination guiding system in which a predetermined path may be followed in the initial stages of flight, utilizing the beam-climber feature in mid-course, and the homing system for the final, or attack phase.

I was still reviewing our argument as I inserted my key in the door of the apartment. I thrust open the door and fumbled for the light switch. Sudden illumination dispelled the darkness, and to my astonishment and alarm I saw two individuals occupying the most comfortable of my chairs. One of these persons held a pistol which he pointed in my direction.

"Close the door silently, doctor, and step inside," said the shorter of the two men.

I stood just over the threshold peering at the two intruders. The one who had spoken, in an almost feminine voice of undoubted culture, was Chinese. He was slender, dressed with expensive taste to the point of foppishness. His face was not forbidding, but genial. I suppose that in his own land he would have been considered handsome by the ladies.

The other man—the one who held the pistol—was his direct antithesis. He was a crude person with a flattened nose and small eyes, that might have been purchased in a secondhand store. His figure was squat, with broad shoulders and thick hands with nails bitten to the quick. "We hope," said the Chinese, "that we did not startle you."

"I admit," I replied, "that I am nonplused. How did you gain admission?"

"My companion," replied the Chinese, "knows about locks." He bowed slightly from the waist. "My name, doctor, is Worthington Ken." He smiled politely. "Do not expect amenities from my companion," he said apologetically. "He has not enjoyed cultural advantages. In addition to which, he is dumb. I do not mean mentally. He was born without the power of speech."

I was striving to compose myself. To walk into one's home and find it occupied by strangers, one of whom exhibits a lethal weapon, does not make for perfect composure. In order to give myself time to resume my habitual mental equilibrium, I resorted to pointless conversation.

"I am an admirer," said I, "of the art of the Chinese people, particularly their ceramics."

"It is gracious of you to say so, doctor. I am an admirer of the material and scientific accomplishments of the United States."

I felt a reservation. "But not," I asked, "of our imponderables—our philosophy?"

"This humble one," he answered, "was honored by being permitted to accompany the Eighth Route Army on its immortal march. It was an ideology inimical to yours that moved me to undergo the hardships involved."

"Then," said I, "you are a Communist."

"If you care to employ that term," he said.

"But," said I, "you have assimilated in speech, in education, in dress, our Occidental civilization."

"Our great philosopher, Ling Po," he answered gravely, "has observed that one may not know the owner of a house by looking at the wall surrounding the garden."

The dumb man made impatient animal sounds. Mr. Ken raised a monitory hand. "If my companion is uncouth you will forgive," he said. He smiled again. "Even his name is uncouth. He is called Bubble Mouth."

"Now," said I, "may I be informed of the purpose of your call?"

"It is unpleasant," said Mr. Ken. "We come to apply pressure. We have enjoyed an intensive education in the art of applying pressure. We were called in for that purpose by our client. Ling Po also has said that the grape does not yield its wine save under the pressure of trampling feet."

"You have been retained," I asked, "to frighten me or, if I fail to respond to duress, to take more violent action?"

"To our infinite regret," said Mr. Ken.

Again the person grotesquely named Bubble Mouth made inarticulate sounds. Mr. Ken shook his head apologetically. "Ling Po also said," he informed me, "that if one is not possessed of a screw driver with which to sink a screw, he must crudely avail himself of a hammer. Bubble Mouth is my crude hammer. Please forgive him."

"Suppose, now," I said, "we come to the point."

"Good manners," said Mr. Ken, "frown upon abruptness. However, sir, I recognize that you will be impatient. I state a fact—namely, that a young lady of beauty named Renee du Guesclin was recently deprived of life."

"True," I said. Somehow it did not seem to me to be possible that this outwardly courtly Chinese gentleman could be dangerous to me. His uncouth companion was more terrifying. His dumbness and the animal sounds he emitted added to this unpleasant impression. As I peered at him, it seemed to me he exhibited terrifying potentialities of brutality.

"Our client," said Mr. Ken in his soft feminine voice, "authorizes us to inform you that he is in a position to assure your conviction for that crime."

"That," said I, "I cannot believe."

"Among other things," Mr. Ken said, "he states that he is able to produce the young woman who served dinner to you and Miss du Guesclin. She will be able to identify you. With other evidence available, your conviction will be certain."

The bleating of the kid had, indeed, attracted the tiger!

The one advantage that rested with me was that these men and their employer believed themselves to be dealing with an unworldly scientist—which possibly I was—who had been suffering from terror since the night of Miss du Guesclin's murder. They would be assured of my ignorance of any counterplot in which I was to be the cat's-paw. They would believe that I would be vulnerable, and they could not know that all the facts of that dire night had been placed by me in the possession of Major Van Tuyl and the FBI. It would be their belief that I would fall a ready victim to blackmail.

It was essential, I conceived, that they should not be disabused of this certainty. To add to their confidence, it would be adroit for me to show apprehension.

"But," I protested, "I did not kill Miss du Guesclin. I assure you I did not."

"'It is more difficult,' says Ling Po, 'for accused innocence to disprove guilt than for the criminal to pull wool over the eyes of the judge.' I fear, in your case, that innocence will not avail."

"Do you mean—you cannot meant—that you would be parties to the conviction of an innocent man?"

"One of the tenets of the ideology which I profess—Communism—is that moral standards cannot prevail where advantage to the cause may be obtained. It is required of us that we be amoral. In the birthplace of Communism many innocent men have been sacrificed on the altar of expediency."

"But in this land," I said, "innocent men never are convicted."

"Oh, doctor," said Mr. Ken regretfully, "you are so mistaken. I could cite instances. Indeed, I myself have been instrumental in the conviction of innocent men."

"Why—why did you come here?" I asked in a shaken voice. "Why are you doing this to me? I have never harmed a soul knowingly. In what manner can I have aroused the anger of Communism?"

"Now, doctor, now, Communism is not inspired by pointless malice. We came to request a favor—a slight favor we thought you might be stubborn about granting. If a door will not yield to gentle pressure, it must be broken."

"What—what," I asked timorously, "are you trying to force me to do?"

"Why, doctor, a thing not difficult. You occupy a very fine and honorable position. A position of trust. A most interesting position, which—shall we say—gives you a high value to our client."

"I occupy," said I, "a position of trust and responsibility."

"So accurate!" said Mr. Ken. "So well stated. A position which places you above suspicion. In this so carefully guarded area, in the White Sands Proving Ground, you can move about at will. You can see and touch and lift. That is true, is it not?"

"To a certain point that is true."

"Let us become hypothetical," he said. "Let us suppose that there existed some quite small object—an object easy to transport. This object is most carefully guarded. Let us further suppose that our client wishes to gain possession of this object. With all the security precautions, guards, identifying badges, it would be quite impossible for one not vouched for to gain entrance to the area, and doubly impossible for him to emerge with the coveted object in his possession."

"It would be impossible," I agreed.

"But not impossible for you," said Mr. Ken. "If, then, you were given a choice between abstracting something from White Sands and being convicted and executed for a murder you did not commit! If such a choice were laid before you, doctor! As a wise man, a man of intelligence, would you not incline to compliance?"

"Look here," I protested. "Be specific. What are you trying to force me to do?"

"There is, we are definitely informed, a device known as the electronic brain. Our client wishes to possess one of these inventions."

"To give it to Communist Russia!" I exclaimed in an appalled voice.

He ignored my exclamation. "It can be carried in a commodious suitcase," he said definitely.

"That," said I, "is highly classified information."

"Little information is kept from us," Mr. Ken said with smugness.

I was striving to think clearly, to determine what course to follow. Suspicion would be aroused if I failed to appear reluctant—to be outraged at a demand that I abstract and turn over to enemy hands the electronic brain. I must protest.

"Do you," I demanded loudly in an angry, excited voice, "realize that what you are suggesting is tantamount to treason?"

"A word," said Mr. Ken soothingly; "a mere word."

"I would be a Benedict Arnold."

"Your history books, which I have studied intently, inform me that General Arnold reached England in safety. Now, in your own case, doctor, we would guarantee that you reached sanctuary across the border in Mexico."

"My answer is no," I said, but not too firmly.

"I feared you might prove stubborn, with mistaken ideas of patriotism, insular ideas. But consider yourself, doctor. You cannot wish to stand before a judge and jury who would surely convict you. The difference, doctor, between being convicted of murder and being accused of treason is that a murderer goes to prison for life or is executed. One accused of treason escapes to a comfortable, well-rewarded and anonymous haven abroad."

"Nothing," I said firmly, "nothing could compel me to betray my country."

The man Bubble Mouth was becoming increasingly restive. He grimaced and babbled. Mr. Ken restrained him with an imperative gesture. I was bringing to bear upon the problem every resource of my intelligence. I was estimating the situation from their point of view. They would not expect me to surrender easily. Indeed, I did not believe they would expect me to surrender at this first demand. To their way of thinking, I was hooked, but it would be incredible if I failed to fight against the hook. A man who has been a decent, law-abiding citizen does not toss aside all he has been brought up to respect and admire in an instant. Not even under duress. The more determined my initial struggle the more natural my conduct would be. Reason told me not to fear for my life. I would be useless to them if I were dead. I resolved to be emphatic.

Before I could speak, Mr. Ken said smoothly, as if an afterthought had occurred to him, "There's another point, sir. There is considerable gossip about you, doctor. About your private life. Shall I say your love life? Though that crude expression may be premature. We learn that your affections are engaged. That there is a young lady who is precious to you."

"Nonsense," I said. "I have no such entanglement."

"We are informed otherwise," Mr. Ken said. He spread his hands. "Unfortunately, we are not permitted to be chivalrous. To us, human beings are merely creatures who are useful or useless. We do not consider sex. I mean to say that sex cannot be a protection."

This Mr. Ken was an incredible human being, suave, dapper, ostentatiously polite. But somehow he made me shudder. He was not inhuman in the way that Bubble Mouth was inhuman, not bestial. His was, rather, an intellectual inhumanity, as if he conceived himself to be above good or evil. He was a robot endowed with intelligence, with will; a mechanical creature without emotions, compunctions, inhibitions or soul.

"The lady's name," said he, "is Miss Melinna Brown. Very, very attractive. A lovely butterfly who emerges from her chrysalis at night."

"What," I asked, "has Miss Brown to do with this matter?"

"You might call her an added inducement," said Mr. Ken gently. "Though she is an innocent bystander, it is possible for an innocent bystander to suffer damage. Sometimes it is profitable to damage an innocent bystander—which you would desire greatly to avert. Oh, yes, doctor, you could so easily insure Miss Brown's safety and happiness. You could also become a hazard in her path. Miss Brown's safety is in the nature of an added pressure."

"Am I to understand," I demanded, "that you are actually threatening harm to Melinna Brown if I decline to betray my country?"

I had not been angry before. I had been appalled by these fearsome men, but I had not been angry at them. I had observed and listened with interest, as belonging to a species I never had observed before. I had felt no rage. But now, unaccountably, something shook me; something welled up within me of a sort I never before had experienced. Not once before in my life had I lusted to attack a man, much less kill him. True, I had found it necessary to use my fists once or twice, but little emotion had accompanied the blows. But now, in a twinkling, everything was blotted out in a red desire to kill. For a moment I was quite blind.

It is fortunate that I am a well-balanced man, not given to moments of emotional instability. Almost at once my blind passion subsided and I was able to think with my usual clarity and efficiency. But I was still angry, with a cold instead of a hot anger. I was even able to wonder why a threatening reference to Melinna Brown should have affected me almost to explosive, hysterical action.

I did find myself, however, in a state of mind which would not be satisfied unless I expressed my self-respect by making my refusal of their proposition emphatic. I did not believe they would shoot me, whatever I said. To do so would admit failure on their part, and bring upon them the censure of their employers.

I arose from the chair in which I had been seated. Bubble Mouth instantly manifested alertness. Mr. Ken smiled in amusement, as at a child.

"Surely, doctor," he said, "you were not planning a breach of hospitality."

I was recalling a point learned long ago in psychology, and later demonstrated by a member of the FBI. Technically, I believe, it is known as time lag. It is the appreciable interval between realizing a situation mentally and sending command from the brain to the hand to perform an action. For instance, a pitcher hurls a ball to the batter. There is a definite interval between the moment when the batter realizes that a pitch has been delivered and the sending of a command from brain to hands to strike. A skilled batsman, as for instance, Mr. Mickey Mantle, possesses more instantaneous reflexes, his time lag is briefer. Hence Mr. Mantle is a superior performer.

I took a provocative step toward Mr. Ken. Both men crouched. Bubble Mouth held his pistol in readiness.

"Now, now, doctor," said Mr. Ken gently. "You surely will not be precipitate." He shook his head warningly. "Bubble Mouth is an adept at the art of pistol whipping."

It was my hope that Bubble Mouth would come close to me. I have been informed that skillful gunmen never allow their victims to come within arm's length. This rule of conduct was not observed by Bubble Mouth. He stepped toward me with animal eagerness, snarling unpleasantly.

"Must we teach you a lesson, doctor?" Mr. Ken said regretfully.

Bubble Mouth thrust forward his pistol so that its muzzle was but inches from my stomach. Quite evidently his purpose was to cow me, having no fear that I would or could make any defensive movement.

I admit I was somewhat troubled about the time lag, never having personally practiced to take advantage of it. But I am not clumsy and my physical movements are well controlled. As the pistol approached my abdomen, the time came for me to put the matter to the test. Then, swiftly, I acted as I had been instructed to do.

With my left hand I knifed viciously down at Bubble Mouth's wrist, putting all available energy into the blow. He was taken utterly by surprise. It turned him half around and his weapon dropped to the rug. This enabled me to grasp his other wrist in the approved manner, whirl him around and apply that wrestler's grip known as the hammer lock. Using him as a battering ram, I propelled him against Mr. Ken so that his head came into violent contact with the abdomen of the Chinese. The result was that both were on the floor in a momentarily helpless position.

I did not hesitate. I found I was strangely enjoying myself and that my rage possessed me again. They were not overweighty men, and I am large, with considerable strength. Before they could untangle themselves I was able to seize each by the nape of his neck and bring their heads together with a gratifying thump. I indulged myself and thumped their heads a second time.

The result gave me satisfaction that amounted to exultation. Bubble Mouth and Mr. Ken lay side by side on the rug and made no effort to move. I found I was guilty of a desire to kick them in the ribs, a quite uncivilized impulse which I restrained.

I did, however, pick up Bubble Mouth's pistol, and, thrusting my hand inside Mr. Ken's coat, I found a second weapon in a shoulder holster, of which I possessed myself. Then I opened the door into the hall. Returning to my victims, I seized each by the collar and dragged them outside, propelling them in the direction of the stairs.

After which I saw to it that my door was locked, and dropped into my chair in a condition of limpness. I was well pleased with myself. In an unaccustomed situation I had acquitted myself with promptness and precision. Under what might be called laboratory conditions, I had demonstrated that the theory of the time lag is sound when put into practice.

I felt the need of a stimulant and supplied the need. The weakness in my knees passed presently. I disrobed and retired, placing the two captured weapons under my pillow. Such was my excited state that I did not fall immediately to sleep.

As I lay wakeful I did some introspection. Among other things, I asked myself a question: Why had a threat of violence to Melinna Brown thrown me into a blind rage of a sort that I had not hitherto believed myself capable of experiencing?

It would have been apparent to a far less discerning mind than mine that matters were approaching a crisis. I suppose that in all human endeavors, be they scientific research or criminal plottings or international wrestlings, a moment arrives when all hangs in the balance. I recall a conversation one evening with two of the world's most eminent physicists. They were discussing the steps which led up to the atomic age in which we find ourselves. One of these gentlemen said to the other, "There was a night which I never shall forget."

"I know," answered the second. "It was the night of the ultimate experiment that would reveal to us whether the bomb could be made a certainty or if it were only a dream."

"Perhaps," said the first, "you will recall the emotions of that night of climax: How every scientist of humanity and integrity who knew what was taking place was praying that the experiment would be a failure."

I was impressed. I was able to comprehend the awesomeness of that hour and the terror it inspired in men's hearts lest they wrest from nature a secret too awful to be entrusted to the hands of human beings.

This petty—by comparison—affair in which I was inextricably enmeshed was swiftly moving toward its climax, and I was afraid.

My telephone rang and I answered. A voice, deep, musical, beautiful in its cadences, asked, "Doctor Gimp, what happened in your apartment just now? It is imperative that I should know."

"On the other hand, it is not, Mr. Thomas," I answered, "imperative that I should tell you."

"Without violation of your obligation of secrecy," said the fat man, "you can answer the questions I shall ask."

"Suppose you ask them first," I replied. "Then I can decide for myself if they may be answered."

"Did two men—a Chinese and a man without the power of speech—call upon you tonight?"

"I found them waiting for me when I opened my door."

"A suave Chinese who quoted Ling Po?"

"Named Worthington Ken," I said.

"Did he make demands upon you?"

"No reply," I answered.

"Was my name mentioned?"

"It was not," I informed him.

"Something happened to those two men," he said. "Something incredible. Can you tell me what it was?"

"Why, sir," I told him, "they exasperated me to a point where I found it expedient to disarm them, rap their heads soundly together and throw them out of my apartment."

"The age of miracles has not passed!" he exclaimed.

"Not a miracle," I told him. "Only a knowledge of that psychological phenomenon known as time lag—the lapse of time between perception and performance."

"I was right," he said as if speaking to himself, "in not underestimating you, doctor. I inform you, sir, that tonight you have coped with the two most capably dangerous men I ever have encountered."

In spite of myself, I liked the repulsive man who was speaking to me. I did not understand him, nor know what was his place in the events which were occurring. But I found him not repulsive to me, save physically. That odd feeling of attraction moved me to speak when, perhaps, I should have maintained silence. But I could not let him go unwarned.

"Mr. Thomas," I said, "I advise you to take precautions for

your safety."

"Meaning what?"

"That the man who procured the throwing of the knife at your back over in Juarez is determined to repeat the attempt upon your life with grim determination to succeed."

"Could you name that man?"

"His name," said I, "is Balthasar Toledo, an art dealer."

"An art dealer indeed!" he exclaimed. Then, after a pause, "I do not comprehend how you know what you seem to know. Men have perished because of less dangerous knowledge. I hope you will be more fortunate."

"Our hopes coincide," I answered.

"I have my faults, Doctor Gimp," he said, "but ingratitude is not one of them. Twice, even three times, you have been of service to me. It may be that in an evil hour I may be able to repay. With one reservation, sir."

"And that?" I asked.

"That," he replied, and I thought, regretfully, "is your removal from life became a sad necessity. But I assure you, doctor, that would come only if it could not be avoided. I wish profoundly, my friend that you had not blundered into this affair."

"I," said I resentfully, "am no blunderer."

"So much the worse," he replied, "for all of us. Good night, doctor. I am obligated to you. As the Spaniards phrase it 'Go with God.' "

I cannot lay my finger on the reason for it, but in that moment I was more keenly afraid of William George Thomas than I was of the Chinese and Bubble Mouth, of the guttural Slav, of Balthasar Toledo. I liked the man, I admired the man, but I perceived in him an infinite, implacable potentiality for evil.

Melinna Brown was among the little knot of people waiting for the bus in the morning. As had become our habit, we occupied the same seat, she beside the window and I on the aisle. Her manner was either restrained or listless—at any rate, for some miles she showed little inclination for conversation. I, myself, had more than enough to think about. It was some time before I realized that she was deliberately trying to make me uncomfortable. I understand that is one of the punitive methods of women—to assume a demeanor which causes the male to become uneasy and wonder what he has done to cause offense. He may have done nothing whatever, but for some perverse reason of her own, the woman desires to make him feel a sense of guilt—doubtless with a view to obtaining some advantage for herself. I determined to give her no satisfaction, but to pretend to be unaware of her mood. It would be a salubrious lesson to her if I impressed her as being wholly unaware that a barrier had been erected between us.

It was not until we approached the administration building that she turned to me brightly and said, "You didn't fool me for a second."

"About what?" I asked.

"About being worried," she said.

"Why should I be worried?" I asked.

"Because I planned it that way," she answered, with a little grimace of self-satisfaction. "Once in a while an application of the silent treatment is good for a man. It makes him quiver."

"I did not quiver," I denied.

She sniffed. "Don't tell me," she said, and then, beaming suddenly, "See you on the bus tonight."

With that, she gathered up her bag and made ready to disembark. I made way for her, handed her down the steps and walked with her to the laboratory. There she went to don the smock which was her daily uniform, and I entered my office. The telephone rang, and it was Major Van Tuyl.

"Can you hop over?" he asked. "I want to show you Exhibit A."

"It will be convenient," I informed him, and, putting on my hat I walked to headquarters and climbed to his office.

"I've had the boys working," he said. "We'll ride over to the Missile Assembly outfit. I want your opinion."

"I was coming to report to you anyhow," I told him.

"Not another caper!" he exclaimed.

"You might call it so," I said, and described last night's

events.

"Hold everything!" he said, and wrinkled his eyelids at me. "Let's get this straight. A couple of gunmen were waiting for you last night?"

"Yes," said I. "I'm informed they are very dangerous men."

"One was holding a gun on you?"

"He committed the indiscretion of approaching too close to me," I said.

"So, with a gun practically against your belly, you disarmed him and roughed the pair of them up."

"It was the time lag, of which I had theoretical knowledge."

"Ain't theory wonderful!" he exclaimed. "Well, well! Maybe you're wasted on science. Maybe you should be doing a man's work. . . . Well, the corn seems to be popping."

He said no more while we drove to the building, where we parked the car. Inside, a lieutenant was waiting for us and took us into a sort of machine shop at the left, where he pointed with some pride to a metal container.

"How's that for false whiskers?" he asked.

"Open her up and let doc take a gander inside," directed the major.

Inside were what seemed to be a mass of electronic devices, recording instruments, delicate wiring and the like. I peered down at it and then glanced inquiringly at Van Tuyl.

"I've seen the electronic brain before," I said.

The lieutenant chuckled. "But never like this," he said. "Give it the once-over."

I knelt and examined the intricate contents of the container. Almost immediately I perceived that something was wrong. It did not make sense. It was a jumble—a skillful jumble, I admit, but to one who had been working daily with the brain, it was nonsense.

"What is this?" I asked.

"How long," countered the major, "would this deceive a layman?"

"Indefinitely."

"How long would it fool a real scientist—an electronics

Johnny?"

"If," said I, "he merely glanced at it, it would deceive him. After a careful examination—if he had not been working on this project—he might have his doubts. To be certain it would be necessary to disassemble."

"And that," said the major gleefully, "will be plenty."

"What is the object of this deception?" I asked.

"To be ready for come what may," he told me. . . . "Much obliged, lieutenant. Swell job. Now we can let the good doctor get back to figuring out how we can knock out Ivan's eye tooth with a flying toothpick."

As we were driving back, the major asked me to repeat in as much detail as possible my conversation with the Chinese and Bubble Mouth. At the end, he remarked with a shrug, "You've made friends and influenced a couple of people. Can you shoot a hand gun?"

"No," I answered.

"Then it would be no use to give you one," he said. "It might just get you in trouble." He shook his head. "Those boys'll never be lighthearted again until they've evened the score. From now on, it'll be a personal thing with them."

"Are you trying to frighten me?" I asked.

"Yes," he said succinctly, and then, "Repeat that about Miss Brown." I did so, repeating the exact words.

He grinned. It seemed no spot for amusement, but Major Van Tuyl had a peculiar sense of humor.

"It was at that point," he said, "that you came to a boil?"

"Yes," I admitted.

"It's a symptom," he said, chuckling, "that you should study. Maybe it means something. I'll get in touch with the FBI, doe. Miss Brown will be properly chaperoned."

I was ironical. "Then she," I asked, "is not expendable?"

"Definitely not. She's been promoted to the status of a reward of merit—a neat little cupcake with frosting to give to a good little boy."

"Major Van Tuyl," I said impatiently, "I haven't time to puzzle out your cryptic observations."

"This," he said, "is a puzzle that will solve itself. In her own good time Nature will open your eyes to see a great rosy light."

For some reason Melinna chose to ride back to El Paso with a young woman from one of the headquarters offices. I occupied a seat with a middle-aged man whose name I did not know. The trip was more tedious than was its wont.

I walked to my apartment, bathed, shaved and sallied forth to dine alone. After I had eaten, I strolled about the streets for an hour, and then went home to don slippers and robe and made myself comfortable to read a brochure about the absorbing topic of cosmic rays. This occupied me until nearly eleven o'clock, at which hour I habitually retire.

My pajamas were on and I was just going to bed when my telephone rang. In the past few days I had come to associate the ringing of my telephone with something of an unpleasant or disturbing nature. So now I walked into the other room and lifted the instrument with some trepidation.

"Hello," I said.

"It's Melinna," said a voice in my ear. "Melinna. I'm frightened. Can you come? Can you come in a hurry?"

"Of course," I answered promptly. "Hold the fort. What—"

Her voice did not speak again, but I heard a thump, as if the receiver had been dropped. There were faint, confused sounds and a cry. "Melinna!" I shouted. "Melinna!"

There was no response. Only silence.

Part Seven

THERE had been something final and conclusive about the thump of Melinna's telephone as it fell. It would be without avail to try to re-establish communication. It must have been dire emergency that had moved Melinna to call to me for help, and it was incumbent upon me to respond with all expedition. Nevertheless, frantic as I was, my brain functioned with its accustomed efficiency. If something was gravely amiss, if the thing that had happened to Melinna had to do with the threat made to me by the Chinese, then it would require more than my unaided efforts to amend it. I lifted the telephone.

"Central," I aid urgently, "this is an emergency call." I gave her the number of the field office of the FBI. "I want speed."

She gave me swift service. Almost instantly I was connected. I wasted no words. "This is Doctor Gimp," I said. "Send men at once to the apartment of Melinna Brown." I gave the address. "Something dire has happened."

Then I ran into my bedroom. I pulled on clothes over my pajamas, donned socks and shoes, and not even pausing to take my hat, I ran down the stairs and continued to run along the street, hoping to find a cruising taxicab. I did not find one. My headlong gait must have astonished what pedestrians I passed, but I did not abate my pace until I arrived breathless at Melinna Brown's address. Two cars stood at the entrance. The FBI was ahead of me.

I took the stairs two steps at a time. The door of her apartment stood open. Two neat young men turned as I entered.

"Doctor Gimp?" one of them asked.

"It is," I said. "Where is Miss Brown?"

"Not here. What's this about?"

"Miss Brown called me for help. I called your office at once."

"When we got here, Miss Brown was gone. Her door stood

open. There are no signs of a struggle. Nothing has been disturbed."

"What do we do?" I demanded.

"We will take care of things here. You will go at once to our office. The special agent in charge is waiting for you. Nothing you can do here, doctor. Our man in the car outside will drive you."

They were right. There was nothing I could do here to assist. These young men were experts, trained as I was not trained, and competent. I descended the stairs again, entered the car in which a driver sat, and was driven to the field office. The special agent in charge was awaiting me. He wasted no time in preliminaries.

"Talk," he said.

I described the brief telephone conversation, consisting as it had of a terrified call for help.

"Yes. Yes," he said. "But before that. I only have things at secondhand. Describe the visit of those gunmen. Their threat with respect to Miss Brown."

I did so, succinctly.

"There is no evidence," he said, "that they suspect you have been working with Major Van Tuyl?"

"They indicated none."

"Excellent," he said. "Their next step will be to get in touch with you. To make demands upon you, using Miss Brown as persuasion."

"One would think so," I answered.

"Then," he said, "you will give them the opportunity to do so. You will go back to your apartment and wait."

"But—" I started to protest.

"You can do nothing to aid Miss Brown. Please do as I request."

"If they contact me? Shall I report to you?"

"No," he said. "Definitely not. We must not risk arousing their suspicions. Everything now depends upon that—upon your being a bewildered and frightened scientist, nothing more. They will demand that you perform certain actions.

They will make threats against Miss Brown's safety to compel you to agree. You will do so."

"I will agree to do what they demand?" I asked.

He nodded in the affirmative. "They will have made a plan. You know what it is they want. What their plan is we do not know, but somehow you are to be used to steal the electronic brain and transport it out of White Sands. In the morning you will go to White Sands as usual. Major Van Tuyl will give you further instructions." He glanced at me keenly. "Major Van Tuyl informs me that you are aware of the risks involved and that you are willing to assume them."

"At the moment," said I, "I seem to be aware of nothing except that Miss Brown is in danger."

"She may," said the special agent in charge, "be suffering discomfort and fright, but she is in no imminent personal danger. She is too valuable alive."

"Yes," I said grimly. "But suppose I do as they demand. Suppose I abstract and deliver to them the electronic brain. How long will Miss Brown live after they have it in their hands?"

"If all goes well," he assured me, "you need have no fear."

"How can you be sure? You cannot be sure."

"Doctor Gimp," he said gravely, "we shall do our best. Much more is at stake than the life of one girl. Perhaps thousands, hundreds of thousands of lives are at stake—the very safety of the United States."

"Another lady who is expendable," I said bitterly.

"In our conception," he answered, "no one is expendable who can be saved. I assure you solemnly, Doctor Gimp, that whatever can be done by human beings to return Miss Brown safely to you shall be done."

"And with that," I said dully, "I must be content."

"We may rely upon you, doctor?"

"I'll go through with it," I answered.

He stood up and extended his hand. "I'm sorry it has come to this," he said. "I'm sorry it had to come to this."

"I warned you to guard her," I said.

"Good night, Doctor Gimp," was all the reply he made to my

accusation.

I thought I perceived the implication, and I was enraged. "Sir," I said, rising to my feet, "if I find that you have deliberately permitted this thing to happen to Miss Brown to further your plans—if harm comes to her in consequence—I shall hold you and Major Van Tuyl accountable."

"Good night, Doctor Gimp," he repeated, and I withdrew from his office.

It was with mingled rage and fear for Melinna's safety that I walked back to my apartment. Yet, looking at the matter from his point of view, from the point of view of one entrusted with the task of averting a calamity from our country, I was compelled to admit that he was right. One life, a dozen lives were as nothing compared to the calamity that might fall upon us if an enemy came into possession of this secret thing. These men, Van Tuyl, the FBI, were not cruel men or ruthless men. Nor is a general who orders his men into battle a cruel or ruthless man. But that reflection made it no less harrowing to me that fate had selected Melinna Brown to be a sacrifice for the common good.

One thing was certain to me, and I judged also to the FBI: I would be approached by the persons who had spirited Melinna out of her apartment. Doubtless contact would be made immediately. It was for that reason that I had been directed to go back to my rooms. It was equally evident to me that all protection would be withdrawn from me to afford unimpeded opportunity.

I proceeded in the direction of my home with a deliberation that did not match my state of mind. At last I reached the vicinity of my apartment house. A driveway stretched back along its northerly side—a tunnel of blackness. As I came abreast of it, a voice, speaking a little above a whisper, addressed me.

"Doctor Gimp," it said insistently.

"Yes?" I replied.

"Step this way," the voice commanded.

"If you want to speak to me," said I, "come out of the darkness."

"We like the darkness," the voice said with a humorous twist.

"It is you again!" I exclaimed, recognizing the voice of Mr. Ken.

"Yes, doctor. But this time we'll know better how to handle you. As Ling Po says, 'Walk wisely in the jungle with open eyes, for a trailing vine may be a venomous asp.' We did not walk wisely before. Please approach."

I obeyed, for I knew they would not be imperative without means to enforce their orders.

"Keep coming," Mr. Ken said, "but stop when I direct."

I was aware of two figures, scarcely discernible in the velvety blackness, also of a metallic object being pressed roughly against my spine.

"Stop," said Mr. Ken. "Do not be alarmed. We have come to give you instructions."

"You have Miss Brown?" I asked, feeling my anger stir.

"We have Miss Brown. An added pressure was needed. We do not like you, Doctor Gimp. You humiliated Bubble Mouth and myself. We have lost face. But we must postpone personal satisfactions. That, we assure you, will come later."

"What," I asked, "do you demand?"

"To start, we will point out the alternatives to refusal. First, you will be convicted of the murder of Miss du Guesclin. Your so-called patriotism might cause you to make that sacrifice for your country. The second alternative is Miss Brown. Unpleasant things will happen to her. We Orientals have a knowledge of methods of inflicting pain."

"I do not doubt it," I said grimly.

"Then, doctor, there is a third alternative: if you are stiff-necked, your usefulness to us is ended. We have, in that case, the permission of our employer to regain our self-respect. Our reputation has been grievously damaged. Personally, we hope you will be stubborn."

An immediate surrender, a too quick and easy surrender, might not be accepted as genuine.

"How," I asked, "can I be guaranteed of Miss Brown's

safety—that she will be released unharmed if I accede to your demands?"

"My word of honor as a Chinese gentleman," said Mr. Ken.

"That is insufficient," I said stoutly.

"Miss Brown will be released intact. Miss du Guesclin never will arise to haunt you." I could sense a shrug in the darkness. "How," he asked, "can we possibly supply a guarantee? You will be compelled, doctor, to take a chance."

The metallic object in the hand of Bubble Mouth pressed more painfully against my back. I stood still a moment, as if hesitating.

"Your decision, doctor?" said Mr. Ken.

"It is Miss Brown," I said in a voice which I hoped expressed misery. "If it weren't for Miss Brown! I—I cannot endure the thought of pain or death for her."

"Now that is very, very reasonable," said Mr. Ken.

"Tell me what you want, Mr. Ken."

"That you can guess, Doctor Gimp. Our objective is the electronic brain."

"But how can I procure it for you?" I asked. "How can I extract it from White Sands? How can I transport it through the gates, past the security guards? It is impossible."

"Not to you, Doctor Gimp. Not to you. You are above suspicion. It will be a matter of simplicity for you. Do you suppose, doctor that we would go so far without a definite, shall we say foolproof, plan?"

"No plan will work," I said firmly.

"We have," said he, "a correct idea of the size of the thing we want, and of its shape. We believe it can be contained in a large suitcase. Right?"

"You are right," I answered slowly.

"So nice of you to be co-operative," said Mr. Ken. "Now here is the expedient. It is simple—beautifully simple. Not tomorrow night, but the night after, you will find some cogent reason for staying at White Sands. Naturally, you will bring with you clothing and toilet articles. You will bring them in a large suitcase—perhaps larger than necessary. But that will arouse no suspicion. You will sleep wherever it is that accommodations are provided. In the morning you will, quite naturally, bring your suitcase to the laboratory where you work and where the electronic brain is kept secure. Am I clear so far?"

"You are clear," I said.

"The rest," said Mr. Ken, "will be as easy as sliding down a pole covered with grease. You will find it necessary to work late—so that you will miss the bus to El Paso. You will borrow a motorcar from the pool. In the meantime you will have been adroit enough to fit the electronic brain into your suitcase. You will put the suitcase in the car and drive yourself to El Paso."

"Possibly," I said, "it can be done."

"You will simply walk out, doctor, suitcase in hand, get into your car and drive, until willing hands deprive you of your burden. Then you will proceed to El Paso, and shortly thereafter Miss Brown will be restored to your eager arms. Can you discover a flaw?"

"None," said I.

"We are forehanded," said Mr. Ken. "Just in case you own no suitable piece of luggage, we have brought one for your use. Do you wish me to repeat these instructions?"

"It will be unnecessary," I said.

"The night after tomorrow. You will be met at a suitable place."

"And allowed to proceed to El Paso?"

"Of course. You will have served your purpose." He chuckled. "And we must not delay your reunion with Miss Brown."

He pressed the handle of a suitcase into my hand. "Good night, doctor, and may good fortune attend you."

With the suitcase in my hand, I proceeded onward to the entrance to my apartment I climbed the stairs, opened my door and turned on the light. The night that lay before me would be sleepless, and I looked forward to it with dread.

To cope with the threat of a personal catastrophe is one thing; to be made responsible for the fate of another is quite different. I am reasonably certain that if it had been only my own life or freedom that was threatened, I would have been able to act with fortitude and integrity. I shall always wonder if I could have acted with equal courage had the choice been given me between betraying my country and saving the life of Melinna Brown.

If my position had actually been as Balthasar Toledo and his accessories had believed it; if I had not been argued into permitting myself to be used as a cat's-paw by Major Van Tuyl; if I had been simply a scientist working in the laboratory of White Sands, how would I have coped with the pressures that had been brought to bear upon me? I confess that I do not know.

But I did not have to make that choice. Events had assumed a form in which I could do nothing but proceed as directed. Nothing was left to my decision, and I could only hope that Major Van Tuyl and the FBI, with which he was associated, knew what they were about and would be successful in carrying out their counterplot. I hoped that in their plan there would be no unexpected geometric angle of yaw, no departure in action from its initial direction in space.

IMMEDIATELY upon my arrival in 'White Sands on the next morning I informed Major Van Tuyl of the events of the night before and of the directions given me by Mr. Ken.

"Tomorrow," he said, "you are to arrive equipped with a suitcase. You are to substitute the electronic brain—which we have prepared—for your clothing and drive with it along the road to El Paso."

"That is correct."

"Somewhere along the way you will be stopped and relieved of your baggage, and allowed to proceed on your way."

"So they told me."

"Did you believe it?"

"No," I said. "I am not so fatuous as to believe that. They will not turn me loose until they have made certain that I have brought them the brain."

He nodded. "Our plans," he said, "are based on that theory. We are certain they will take you and the brain to that hideout in the Organ Mountains. For what other purpose would they have set up that advance post? You and the brain will disappear. What safer place to hide you than up at that prospect hole? Give them a safe spot—and time—to examine the contraption to see if it is the real thing. Then, at their leisure, they can transport it across the border."

"A point of personal interest to me," I said uncomfortably, "is what becomes of me when they're satisfied I've performed my mission. They're not," said I, using a favorite word of my mother's, "persnickety about taking human life. They've killed the Mexican, Iturbe, on the train; they have murdered the two prospectors; they have eliminated Renee du Guesclin. I will have served my purpose. I will be only an encumbrance."

"You," Van Tuyl assured me, "are included in the precautions we have taken."

"I hope they will be effective," I said, and he grinned wryly. "I think," I said after a pause, "that I should like to write a couple of letters—in case. One to mother and one to Miss Melinna Brown."

"Naturally," he said. "I'll see they are delivered. In case."

I fear I was of very little use to Doctor Newcomb or the laboratory that day. To concentrate on matters scientific was beyond my powers, and the minutes dragged. That night my sleep was fitful. In the morning I carried the empty suitcase to the laboratory. Van Tuyl came over and together we fitted the counterfeit brain into it. Its dimensions were somewhat smaller than the interior of the bag, so we packed it carefully with newspapers. It was, of course, heavier than my clothing, but not so heavy that I could not carry it comfortably.

I continued to follow directions, delaying my departure until the bus was gone. A car was brought over from the pool and parked in front of headquarters. Van Tuyl was there to see me off. Rather to my surprise, he laid aside his gruff mannerisms. He seemed almost solicitous. After we had placed the suitcase in the rear seat of the automobile, he went so far as to extend his hand.

"Well, so long, doc," he said. "I hope it falls butter side up."

I handed him the two letters I had written, and he nodded.

"I'll return them to you tomorrow," he said.

"Right," I answered.

He shook hands again and scowled. "I've met worse guys than you, doc," he said. "Be on your way."

I drove out of the circle and headed southward for El Paso. Though I did not turn to look, I knew that he was standing there peering after me. I drove out on the road that passed the swimming pool and the launching sites and the building that housed miracles of electronics. I glanced sidewise at the radar saucers upon its roof and wished that they or some of the marvelous devices on the floor below could be able to keep track of my progress as they did of the progress and behavior of missiles launched from the sites at my left. But no instrument had been devised that could give that service. I was on my own.

My badge carried me past all security guards and barriers. Over at my right loomed the fastnesses of the Organ Mountains. I did not drive to U.S. Route 54, but took the desert road, which cut off several miles of distance. Presently I would cross the southern line of New Mexico into Texas. I passed no cars. The desert stretching about me was deserted and dusk commenced to descend upon the loneliness. I drove slowly, expecting now to be accosted and stopped.

As I skirted a low sand hill a man stepped into the road and held up his hand. It was the Chinese, Mr. Ken. He was courteous and said "Good evening" as if it were a chance encounter. I made no response.

"Have you the gadget?" he inquired.

"On the back seat," I said.

"Any difficulties?"

"None," I replied.

He turned, waved his hand, and Bubble Mouth appeared, driving a car from its place of concealment over the hard floor of the desert. He stood, mute and dour. I saw no firearms, but imagined them to be present in places of accessible concealment. The two men lifted the suitcase from my car, transferring it to their own.

"I've performed my part," I said.

"Well—nearly, doctor."

"I was to be allowed to proceed to El Paso," I said.

"You didn't get it in writing," said Mr. Ken. "We can't bear to part with you so soon."

I protested as a matter of form, but they compelled me to alight and take a seat beside Mr. Ken, who was driving their car. Bubble Mouth guided my car off the road and behind the dune, where it could not be seen. They were very matter of fact about it all. Bubble Mouth returned and climbed into the rear seat.

It was my expectation that they would take one of the desert roads which were little more than tracks toward the Organs. That was what Van Tuyl and I had been certain they would do. But, to my surprise and consternation, they proceeded onward for a time and then, instead of turning to the right, they veered onto a track that led toward Alamogordo. I knew instantly that something had gone wrong with Van Tuyl's planning—dreadfully wrong. We were not driving toward the Organ Mountains and the mine of the two prospectors, but in exactly an opposite direction. All counterplans had been predicted upon the Organ Mountains. We had been tragically in error.

Boldly they crossed the pavement of Route 54.

"If," said Mr. Ken, "anybody meddles with us, be ready with your badge and conversation."

But no one meddled with us. We crossed the railroad and, as darkness fell, were close to the eastern wall of mountains.

"You'll be interested," Mr. Ken said, "to know that we are entering the great state of Texas."

I was not interested; I was thoroughly alarmed.

"Where," I asked, "are we going?"

"Nice place. With a view of the river. Not much of a river, we admit, but it's the best we have. You'll be able to look over into Mexico. Ever hear of a wetback, doctor?"

"I believe it is argot denoting Mexicans who enter this country illegally."

"Go to the head of the class," said Mr. Ken. "It's one of the spots where wetbacks get their backs wet, when there's water enough."

There was rough going and discomfort, but the car proceeded without mishap. Although it was growing dark, the driver turned on no headlights. He seemed to drive by instinct. At last, after what seemed hours of jolting and slewing, we approached a mass blacker than the darkness of the night. We passed through a gate in a wire fence and the mass of blackness disclosed itself to be an adobe house of some dimensions.

"No place like home," said Mr. Ken. "Down with you, doctor, and prepare to be received in due form."

At the sounds of our arrival, a door opened and closed again and a man walked toward us. We had arrived—not at a mine in the Organ Mountains about which Major Van Tuyl would have thrown a cordon of men, but at a house many miles away from that spot about which no cordon could have been thrown, because Major Van Tuyl was unaware of its existence. Intelligence and security, of which Van Tuyl was the chief, and the FBI, with whom he co-operated, had been outwitted. In that moment I gave up hope.

The man who emerged from the house approached the car.

"Well?" he demanded. I recognized the voice of Balthasar Toledo.

"A most successful enterprise," said Mr. Ken. "Our amiable friend, Doctor Gimp, consented to accompany us."

"Where is it?" Toledo asked impatiently.

"Resting innocently on the back seat," Mr. Ken responded. "The excellent Bubble Mouth will lift it out."

The dumb man got down, opened the door of the car and lifted out the suitcase containing the bogus electronic brain. Toledo seized it avidly. He spoke to me.

"For your sake, Doctor Gimp," he said, "I hope this is what we want. I trust you have not been so unwise as to offer a substitute. Come in the house."

It would have been useless to protest or to resist. No sooner was I standing on the ground than Toledo struck me viciously with his fist, knocking me against the side of the car. "Just the first payment on a debt!" he snarled.

"And when," asked Mr. Ken, "is the privilege to be granted to me to restore my own honor?"

"Business first," Toledo said, and pushed me toward the black bulk of the house.

I entered a large square room, its ceiling supported by unhewn logs. The illumination was kerosene lamps. A fire burned cheerfully in a huge fireplace, but it did not cheer me. As we stepped into the room a man arose from a chair by the fire, and I recognized the guttural person whom Melinna and I had seen in the box canyon in the Organs with Toledo. "That iss id?" he asked eagerly. "Let me see. Let me examine." He shook his round head uneasily. "I cannot believe yet. In the end, after all the so hard work and planning, it was so easy!"

He bent over the suitcase avidly. A suppressed excitement settled upon the room. He lifted out the aluminum container and raised its lid. Inside was disclosed a mass of complicated wires, dials, electronic devices, over which the Slav bent with narrowed eyes.

"Id iss delicate. Id iss complex. Yess, yess. Complex. I belief this iss id. I believe we have id in our hands. But iss too delicate, too much science for me." He raised his head and stared at me venomously. "I cannot be sure. I must wait for him to come. He will know—he, our greatest man in this thing of electronics. Only he can make the guarantee id iss genuine." He stood erect and peered from man to man. "If this iss id," he said, and his stature seemed to increase, "we deserve well of our country."

"I trust," Toledo said grimly, "we do more than deserve. I trust there will be prompt payment."

"Of that you shall have no doubt," said the guttural man.

"In America," said Mr. Ken, "there is a saying. It is a cogent saying. Not florid but to the point. Cash on delivery. Now I, Worthington Ken, am a convinced and practicing and loyal Communist. But I do as other Communists do, even the highest. I spare a thought for my own advantage. So I repeat, cash on delivery. Also, no cash in hand, no delivery."

The guttural man threw back his shoulders and his eyes glittered with the fire of fanaticism. "The bargain was made," he said sternly. "It will be out-carried. Do you dare to question?"

"I am not a timid man," Toledo said crisply. "You are still on American soil, Otto. These are my men. Don't throw your Soviet weight around. The deal was to be C.O.D."

"Understood," Otto said, still arrogant. "Payment awaits the coming of him. He will examine. He will pay." He looked about him scornfully. "I do not accomplish this thing for money. Now we conquer the world. Now we smash the democracies of blood-sucking plutocrats. Now comes the war—the people's war. We conquer the world."

Mr. Ken watched placidly, his Chinese features expressionless. Bubble Mouth stood stolid, a menacing figure.

"What says Ling Po?" asked Mr. Ken. " 'TAhe hungry man is a sword without a blade.' We have not eaten."

"Manuel!" shouted Toledo, and a Mexican came into the room from what was doubtless the kitchen.

Toledo spoke imperatively in Spanish, which I did not understand. The Mexican vanished, to return presently with eating utensils, which he placed upon the long, wooden table. He disappeared, to return again with a great pot of beans and a bowl of chili and a pot of coffee.

Mr. Ken turned to me with geniality. "Our house is yours, and all within it. I have longed to see the sight of a condemned man eating a hearty meal."

"The implication," said I steadily, "does not improve my appetite."

" 'The brave man,' says Ling Po, 'faces death as if it were but a pleasant journey,' " Mr. Ken said.

Toledo was abrupt. "When," he demanded, "does your scientific nabob arrive? I want to get this thing out of my hands, across the border, tonight. I want to be a long way from here before morning—a long way into the interior of Mexico."

"He should be here now," said Otto.

We sat at the table. "I hope the chili will not be too hot for you, doctor," Toledo said ironically.

Bubble Mouth ate voraciously; Mr. Ken ate daintily. There was a light in the latter's black eyes which in an Occidental would have been the light of mischief. He seemed to take a sort of elfin satisfaction in suggesting an unpleasant possibility.

"Now that the cup is near the lip, honored employer," he said to Toledo, "I would ask if the name of William George Thomas has given you uneasiness."

"Damn William George Thomas," Toledo said with sudden rage.

"Remember," said Mr. Ken softly, "what he did to you in Budapest. When, also, the cup was near the lips. Remember Harbin. Let your mind recall Cairo. Me, I never forget that William George Thomas is in El Paso."

Otto's guttural voice spoke gratingly. "I gave the order that this fat man be kill," he said, glaring at Toledo. "Him I fear more than all the FBI. That man so fat he almost cannot move, but with the subtle brain."

"This fat man," said Mr. Ken admiringly, "he can move when movement is necessary. I think he could run a hurdle race if circumstances required."

Uneasy silence fell upon the room. The Mexican came in to clear away the dishes. He passed close to Toledo, who kicked at him viciously, as if he must have some outlet for the vile temper he was in. Manuel avoided the kick in a lazy, placid way, as if such unpleasant gestures were an expected part of his day's work. He gathered up the plates and knives and forks, and slouched back into the kitchen.

"You two," said Toledo, surrendering again to poisonous temper, "haven't covered yourselves with glory. You, Ken, and Bubble Mouth have left the fat man alive to worry us." He tapped himself on the chest. "When I have a job to do, I do it. Where would we have been if I hadn't taken care of that Mexican secret-service man on the train?" The serving man had reached the kitchen door. He paused an instant and then disappeared.

"Is it time to boast?" asked Mr. Ken. "What you did was neat. But were not Bubble Mouth and myself competent in the affair of Renee du Guesclin?"

"Anyone can kill a woman!" snarled Toledo.

"Not with such embellishments," protested Mr. Ken. "Not

with adroitness that put Doctor Gimp so securely in our hands. Nor were we incompetent when we gave Miss Brown a pressing invitation to be my guest."

I was appalled. Here we sat in one room, five of us; I a prisoner, but with ears to hear. In my presence they spoke openly of their crimes, as if it were of no consequence that I should be a witness. The implication was plain. It was not their intention that I ever should be able to testify.

"It was your promise to me," I said, "that if I abstracted the electronic brain, Miss Brown would be set at liberty, unharmed. Where is Miss Brown? Do you mean to live up to that part of your agreement?"

"I fear," said Mr. Ken, "you failed also to have that clause reduced to writing." He shrugged and glanced sidewise at Balthasar Toledo. "Our friend is annoyed with Miss Brown. She rejected his blandishments. I fear he will insist upon completing unfinished business with the Lady."

"I suppose it would be futile," said I, "to point out that she cannot harm you. That she has no knowledge that can harm you."

"Quite futile to point out," said Mr. Ken. "But I fancy Miss Brown has wherewith to extricate herself. Mr. Toledo will be in funds. He will be opulent and need not economize. Let us say that if Miss Brown were complaisant—if she should consent to become Toledo's traveling companion—to save herself from death by accepting, as the sentimental novelists express it, a fate worse than death?"

I knew his intention was to torture me with a device more harrowing than the Chinese Death of a Thousand Deaths. I felt blind rage surge up within me again, the lust to kill. But I was helpless. I ground my teeth.

"Perhaps," said Mr. Ken in his modulated voice, "you would like to see Miss Brown."

He walked to a door at the right of the kitchen door and pulled it open. "Come out, Miss Brown. It is visiting hours. A friend has come to see you."

Melinna stepped into the room, followed closely by a large woman of Indian extraction with gleaming eyes, dusky skin and high cheek bones. Melinna stood staring at me, wide-eyed, pale but resolute. When she spoke, I was aghast, for it seemed to me that her words, if not her manner, indicated that the treatment she had received, the terror she must have endured, had caused her mind to become instable.

"Alt, Doctor Gimp! In servomechanisms," she said, as if delivering a lecture, "there is a signal applied to the control circuit that indicates any misalignment between the controlled and controlling members. This is known as an error signal. Can you tell me, doctor, if such a signal can, in science, be designated as female?"

She paused an instant, and then went on gravely, "An oscillograph would be so very, very useful, doctor. You haven't one in your baggage, by any chance?"

"Melinna!" I exclaimed. "Melinna!"

Before I could say more, before she could utter more electronic jargon, the Indian woman seized her by the shoulders and thrust her back into the room in which she had been confined.

"What," demanded Toledo, "was all that about?"

"The lady," said Mr. Ken, "would appear to have burst her mental buttons."

That was my first unhappy impression. But her eyes had been steady and clear and sane. Was it possible, I asked myself, that by using verbiage incomprehensible to our captors, she had sought to convey some message to me? If so, what could it be? An error signal. Could an error signal be female? A signal indicating misalignment between controlling and controlled members. Was there some misalignment between the human members of this group? Was she herself, being female, an error signal? And an oscillograph! An oscillograph is an instrument for making a record of rapidly varying electric quantity. She had said that I would find one useful. There would be, if my assumption was right and she was conveying a message, some rapid change in circumstances which I should note and of which I might take advantage.

For the first time I felt the faint stirrings of hope. I was certain that Melinna intended to give me hope. But then I remembered the imminent arrival of the awaited Soviet electronic scientist who would be able to examine the bogus electronic brain and pronounce upon its genuineness. Such slender hope as had blossomed withered and died.

My situation was critical. At any moment the Soviet electronic expert might arrive. For a man of his undoubted attainments but a short time would be required for him to detect the bogus character of the electronic brain which I had delivered to these people. Their reaction would be swift and savage.

The plans of Major Van Tuyl had been based upon a false assumption. The frustration of Communist agents and my own safety had been predicated upon the assumption that Balthasar Toledo and the man Otto would take me to their advance post in the Organ Mountains. It had been a reasonable assumption, for why otherwise would they have murdered two prospectors and established themselves there, if not to possess an easily accessible spot for this very purpose?

They had not outthought Major Van Tuyl, because they could not have known of our knowledge of their possession of the mine. It was simply that we had misread their plans—with dire consequences.

I have often wondered what thoughts passed through the mind of condemned man in the interval of waiting to be led to the place of execution. Now I was in a position to state that his thoughts were not pleasant. It is difficult for a man to realize that his hours are numbered. It was difficult for me to accept that fact. I suppose that hope is the one indestructible emotion of man, otherwise he could not continue to exist. We are aware of tragedies on every hand, but we are confident that calamity is a thing that happens to others, never to ourselves. Even now, a prisoner in this room, surrounded by men to whom human life meant nothing, I could not bring myself to accept my fate. I would continue to hope that something would intervene before it was too late for intervention.

I was afraid, but I was gratified to observe that it was not with a groveling terror. I resolved, and believed I would be able to keep my resolution, that I would face the end with dignity.

My thoughts turned to Melinna Brown and I was tortured by the realization that, but for me, she would not be imprisoned in the adjoining room. I was conscious of a desire to see her, to speak with her, to express to her my grief that it was I who was to blame for her situation. And there was something else I wished to say to her, a disclosure I desired to make. It was unendurable to pass out of life without saying certain words to her.

That desire became so strong that I resolved to ask for the granting of this favor. I turned to Toledo.

"Mr. Toledo," I said, "I wish to speak to Miss Brown."

"No," he answered.

"It can do you no harm," I said. "To you it will be a very slight thing."

Mr. Ken smilingly intervened. "Listen to the wisdom of Ling Po," he said. " 'He who grants a boon to an enemy gains merit. The man who sows a handful of rice in the soil of his foe may eat of the harvest in the day of his own starvation.' Even we Chinese, Mr. Toledo, could devise no more subtle torture than to grant a final interview between condemned lovers."

Toledo frowned, then shrugged. He motioned toward the door behind which Melinna was imprisoned.

I accepted this as permission. No one interfered with me as I walked across the room and opened the door. Melinna was sitting before a smaller fireplace, warming herself at its blazing logs. The Indian woman crouched on the floor.

"They have let me see you, Melinna," I said.

She turned her head and was able to smile. "We're in a pretty mess," she said.

"It is my fault," I said. "I'm to blame. I want you to know how bitterly I accuse myself."

"Don't be silly," she said tartly. That certainly was not the lofty language of high tragedy. It was down to earth. She grinned in that impish manner that was hers. "You didn't invent sin," she said.

"Did you," I asked, "convey some message to me?"

She put her finger to her lips. "You understand plain English, don't you?" She made a moue. "So," she said, narrowing her eyes, "does this chaperone of mine." It was a warning.

"I," said I, "had a special reason for asking permission to see you."

"Most men have," she said.

"It is possible, indeed probable," said I, "that I shall not survive this night. There was a thing I did not wish to leave unsaid."

"In those circumstances," she answered, "I probably should listen."

"Aren't you afraid?" I asked.

"Of what you're going to say, or of things in general?"

"Of the situation in which we find ourselves," I said gravely.

"I'm scared out of my wits," she answered. "Do you want me to throw a wing-ding?"

"It is not a time for flippancy," I reproved.

"Flippancy," she retorted, "is as apt to the occasion as pedantry. Me, I'd rather pass out with a quip on my lips than demonstrating my higher education. Do you have to talk like a textbook? If, just once, you would use a short, ordinary, commonplace word instead of reciting in multisyllables, you would get favorable mention by the committee." She waggled her head disparagingly. "All right, doctor, proceed with your oration."

"You make it difficult," I told her. And then proceeded. "There was," said I, "a long interruption in our acquaintanceship—from childhood to maturity. As a little girl you exerted a profound influence upon me and caused a definite modification in my life. Unexpectedly, we made contact again, and though you have irritated me and confused me, I find that you still are potent to influence me and to modify me. I may say that I have been disconcerted to discover the place of importance you have usurped in my life, and that, without volition on my part—indeed against my firm resolution—I have become obsessed by affectionate regard for you. To the point, Melinna, where you have become paramount in my thoughts to the extent that a future in which I would be dissociated from you is definitely appalling. It was to tell you this that I begged for permission to speak with you tonight."

She stared at me. Her lips parted. It might almost be said that she gawped at me in astonishment.

"Well," she said breathlessly, "I'll be damned!"

"I have made my meaning clear," I said.

"That," she answered, "is what you think!" Suddenly she was angry. "Listen, you big, pedantic lunk! Any girl with the normal equipment of arms and legs—and mine are very nice legs—looks forward to the time when some man shall tell her she is the apple of his eye. It's a glorious, whopping, heart-busting moment, and it should be done with trimmings."

"Indeed?" said I.

"And what do I get? Do you get all churned up with emotion and blurt? A girl can like that. Do you just forget about words and grab? That's a dandy method. Do you get all fussed and have to have it pried out of you? Which could be fun. No, you mount the platform, lay out your notes on the reading desk and declaim a tiresome valedictory oration. When I sort it out I get the vague and unemotional idea that you are proposing to me. You inundate me with a spate of two-dollar words to the number of a couple of hundred, when an illiterate truck driver with a split lip could say it better in three one-syllable words. You've turned a big moment into a calamity!" She was flushed and furious.

"What three one-syllable words?" I asked helplessly.

"You'll never know!" she snapped.

Would I never know? I regarded her with something like despair. I had endeavored honestly to express to her my sentiments: to declare to her, in fitting terms, how precious she was to me. As one of the final acts of my life I had striven to inform her that in all the world was no other woman but her, and that I cherished her far beyond all other living things. To my consternation, she showed in return nothing but resentment. I had indeed proved inadequate to a crucial situation. I found myself angry—angry at her and at myself. I was shaken by emotion to the point of unstudied action and incoherence.

I strode toward her, seized her by the shoulders and shook her roughly, glaring down into her astonished eyes. Speech seemed to be wrenched from me.

"Damn it to hell, you little snip!" I said furiously, "I love you!"

"By golly!" she exclaimed, and her face flushed and her eyes glowed. "You've got the makings, after all!"

Her lovely hands reached for me. I found myself lifting her in my arms and crushing her lips to mine. It was an exhilarating experience. "Sweetheart!" I mumbled. "Sweetheart!"

She released herself and stood breathing in gasps. She was radiant, beautiful, desirable. She pushed me away.

"You did fine!" she said. "I'll make something of you, darling! My dumb darling! Now scram out of here. Love isn't the next order of business."

I strode out of the room in a mood of exultation. I closed the door after myself and became aware of Toledo, of Mr. Ken's Oriental face, of the brutish face of Bubble Mouth, and of the Eastern European, Otto. The Mexican cook was standing in the kitchen door.

"Lipstick," said Mr. Ken, "was unknown to Ling Po or he would have made a wise saying about it."

Before any other man could speak or move to deride or to threaten, a roughly clad man I never had seen before, burst into the room.

"A car's comin'," he said. "From El Paso way."

"Get back outside," Toledo said imperatively. "Station the men." The man slammed the door after him.

"Could it be he?" Mr. Ken asked.

"Not from El Paso," said Otto. "He comes across the river. Horseback."

"This," said Ken softly, "I do not like."

We listened. There was no shot. A motorcar drove into the yard and stopped before the door. Toledo, pistol in hand, snatched the door open and stood on the tiny porch. Bubble Mouth and Mr. Ken, also displaying arms, stood beside him. I strained to look over their shoulders at the automobile. Its rear door opened and an enormous, elephantine figure emerged with glacierlike slowness. The four men on the porch stood as though frozen.

"Good evening, gentlemen all," said the musical voice of William George Thomas. "The time seemed clement for me to intervene to cast a stone into the pond with attendant ripples. Replace your weapons, gentlemen; there is subject matter for us to debate."

With the ponderous movements of a pachyderm, William George Thomas crossed the intervening space and mounted the step. Placidly he shouldered aside the men who stood there, entered the room in which I stood, calmly selected a chair and lowered his weight into it.

"Good evening, doctor, good evening," he said to me. Then to Toledo, "Surely, my old friend," he said, "you aren't surprised to see me, now that matters approach their climax. Surely you're not surprised."

No one moved. No one spoke. The fat man gazed blandly about him, unmoved as if he sat in the safety of his own apartment.

"Will someone," he asked politely, "offer me a cigarette?"

Part Eight

WILLIAM George Thomas expressed nothing but benignity as he settled himself comfortably in the creaking chair. His small eyes beamed over dumpling cheeks as he puffed contentedly at his cigarette. His was the manner of a man sure of a warm welcome, and his aplomb served well to arouse the apprehension of Toledo and of the very intelligent Mr. Ken. Here was something they could not appraise.

The adipose man had come alone. Nonchalantly he had waddled into the lion's den. He radiated confidence—the confidence of a man who held a known advantage. I, a spectator, was aware of the uneasiness of my captors; I could almost read their minds.

William George Thomas, with what seemed like incredible recklessness, had come to this spot alone; had placed himself in the hands of men who he knew well had sought to take his life. I could see that they were shaken. It was incredible to them that the fat man should have ventured as he had ventured unless he had the whip hand. They were thrown off balance. William George Thomas was relishing the situation.

"Doctor Gimp," he said suavely, "you seem to be in a predicament."

"I am, indeed," I said.

"I assume," he said, "that the delectable Miss Brown shares your uncomfortable dilemma?"

"She also is here," I told him.

"I trust," he said, letting his eyes move from face to face, "that she has been treated as befits a charming lady, and that you yourself have suffered no ill usage."

"Miss Brown," I answered, "has not been molested. As for me, with the exception of one unwarranted blow by Mr. Toledo, I have taken no harm."

He nodded. "We will consider the unwarranted blow later," he said. He pointed to the open suitcase and the counterfeit electronic brain. "That contraption," he said, "I assume is the objective of all the gyrations and maneuverings. One would scarcely credit that so much lethal potentiality could be compressed in so constricted an area. Who," he asked with a suave smile, "could conceive that world dominance could be stored in so small a package?"

"If I lifted a finger," Toledo said in a grating voice, "Bubble Mouth would shoot you where you sit."

"But you will not lift that finger," Mr. Thomas said, with a faint smile.

"What will stop me?" Toledo asked.

"Your uncertainty," explained Mr. Thomas, "as to what the consequences would be. I am a devious man, Balthasar, as your previous experience of me has taught you. I vanish and I appear. It may seem that I do this or omit that without rhyme or reason. But you have unhappy knowledge that I neither act nor refrain from acting without a purpose." He made a deprecating gesture. "My superiority to you, Balthasar, lies in the realm of higher intelligence. I am a vain man, but my vanity is soundly based."

"Stop gabbling and talk business," Balthasar Toledo said.

Mr. Ken smiled blandly. "We Orientals," he said, "also have devious intelligence."

"I admire you, Mr. Ken," William George Thomas said, with a gracious nod. "But you are hampered by Balthasar's ineptness."

"Have you considered that I am a fatalist, sir?" Mr. Ken asked. "True, Mr. Toledo might be deterred by thoughts of the consequences of shooting you. I would not. In this matter I have lost face. Which is unendurable to one of my lineage. If I thought face would be restored by shooting you, I would not hesitate."

"Still," said Mr. Thomas, "you will not shoot. There are other considerations than fatalism and face." He smiled widely. "There is cash."

"You came to talk about cash?" demanded Toledo.

"In part. My tastes are expensive and my expenses high."

"You want to bargain?"

"With some extra exertion I could take all," Mr. Thomas said. "But I will dicker. There are times when it is wise to take half a loaf—if the loaf is big enough." He indicated the aluminum container. "You have a thing there. It is ready for delivery to your employers. But there is a question. Will your employers pay you your fee for a pig in a poke? I am almost omniscient, but I do not know if what you have is the electronic brain or a useless mass of wires and dials and other plausible gadgets."

"Id iss genuine," said Otto harshly.

"You are not competent to pass upon that," the fat man said with no lack of courtesy. "Your Kremlin employers will not purchase save on the opinion of the highest scientific authority."

"Who," said Toledo, "is due to arrive at any moment."

"It will be dangerous for him to cross the border. He and his superiors will be resentful if he takes that risk for a counterfeit. My experience with Communist gentlemen is that they express their resentment vigorously. They liquidate."

"Do you think it is bogus?" demanded Toledo.

Thomas waggled his huge head. "If I knew that, I would have saved myself this journey. I do not know. I am compelled to act as if the thing were genuine. But, gentlemen, I have taken into reckoning an imponderable factor which has escaped you."

"What factor?" demanded Toledo.

"I am a rare judge of human beings," said William George Thomas with a manner almost fatuous.

"What has that to do with it?" Toledo demanded.

"Doctor Gimp," said he, "has impressed me favorably. I am not prejudiced in his favor because he saved my life. My opinion is due to observation."

"You're talking in circles," said Toledo.

"I am talking in a straight line. You have based your entire plot upon the assumption that all men can be bought. By cash, by favor, by self-preservation. A very wide experience has taught me that this assumption is not true. It is very bad for our business, we who live in the half-world and whose standards are those of amorality. It is a stumbling block in our path that there do exist men of integrity who cannot be swayed by any pressure imposed by man."

"Put it in clear words," said Toledo.

"Why, gentlemen, I pay Doctor Gimp the high compliment of believing that his integrity is without flaw. There's your imponderable."

"You think he has tricked us?"

"I think it probable he has bamboozled you."

"Absurd," Toledo said. "He knows that would mean his death. He knows it would mean the death of this girl in the other room. He would be deliberately walking into a bullet. No man would do that."

"Since the dawn of history," the fat man said, "a great many men have sacrificed their lives deliberately for a smaller thing than is involved here. And the lives of those dear to them. It is a thing to reckon with. It is a thing, I fear, that men of your persuasion fail to consider. I preach no sermons, I make no prophecies, but if your ideology, the ideology of Communism, crashes into ruin, it will not be guns that cause it, nor guided missiles. Nor armies nor navies. The weapon against which you will not be able to prevail is a basic integrity among mankind, more widespread than you know, which not yield to cajolery, to temptation or to force." He paused, and then added gravely, "Sometimes I have wished I myself were a man of integrity."

Mr. Ken sneered. "In your Western mythology is a fallen angel named Lucifer. He never is depicted as fat to grossness."

Mr. Thomas nodded, and somehow that gesture frightened me. There was that in it which was notable and grim. "Until that moment, Mr. Ken," he said, I have felt no personal enmity toward you."

"Damn it!" exclaimed Toledo. "Stop the stupid orations and come to the point! What have you got to trade?"

It was a state of reluctant truce on the part of my captors. They were armed and had retainers outside. If William George Thomas carried a weapon, it was not in evidence. Whether his presence was an advantage or a disadvantage to me, I could not guess; for some illogical reason, I was hopeful. To Balthasar Toledo's question, he replied, "I shall suggest no proposal until the arrival of your scientist. When he pronounced upon the authenticity of that object, I will suggest a treaty. And state what my side of the bargain will be." He smiled about him. "Is there nothing to drink?" he asked.

Toledo shouted for Manuel, who appeared from the kitchen. "Whisky, ice and water," Toledo ordered. The Mexican set forth bottle, glasses, a bowl of ice and a pitcher of water.

"'Eat, drink and be merry,'" quoted Mr. Ken suggestively.

"It is not I who shall die," said Mr. Thomas.

There was such tension in that room as I had never experienced. Yet William George Thomas did not seem to share it. The uncouth Bubble Mouth stood against the wall, uttering from time to time impatient, animal sounds. His posture was the crouch of a gunman, and his right hand did not leave the holstered pistol on his hip. Whatever of suavity Toledo had possessed was no longer visible. Otto sat as if bewildered, and Mr. Ken prowled up and down, as graceful and menacing as a hungry cat. Manuel, when his service was completed, did not return to the kitchen, but leaned against the frame of the door indolently, his eyes half closed, as if he slept standing up. It was a strained atmosphere which could not long exist without explosion.

Again the door was opened and the same man who had announced the coming of William George Thomas thrust his head into the room. "Horses," he said succinctly. "From the direction of the river."

"Let them come on. Keep them covered in case," Toledo said, and sighed with relief. "It will be our man."

Presently we could hear the fall of hoofs, then voices, and the sound of feet mounting to the porch. The first to enter was a tall wiry man of some sixty years, dressed in riding boots and breeches and coat as if for a canter in Central Park. His forehead was lofty, his eyes a brilliant gray, his nose straight and patrician. He paused to accustom his eyes to the light.

"I," he announced formally, "am the Herr Doktor Rudolf Von Steen."

A German, not a Russian! I should not have been surprised, for Russia had commandeered some of the best of Germany's scientific brains to work in its laboratories. The name was not familiar to me.

"You are late," said Toledo.

"There were difficulties," said the Herr Doktor, speaking without accent. "You have been successful?"

"There it is," Toledo said, pointing.

Von Steen's eyes glowed. His expression was, it seemed to me, more that of a scientist avid to study the results of some epoch-making experiment than that of a political fanatic hoping to possess a fabulous weapon of war.

"Place it on the table," he commanded arrogantly. "Fetch more light. Stand back that I may examine."

"A few preliminaries first," said Toledo dryly.

"What are these preliminaries?"

"Payment for services rendered," said Toledo.

"Do you expect payment before a thorough examination?" Von Steen said scornfully. "You are not dealing with fools."

"But you have it with you."

"Again I say you are not dealing with fools. The money is at hand, convenient, well guarded."

My moment was upon me. How long the bogus electronic brain could deceive the intelligent, informed eyes of Doctor Von Steen I could not guess. It had been well constructed, with art and skill. Perhaps he would not be able to detect the deception for five minutes, a quarter of an hour, an hour. But of one thing I was certain. When he arose to his full height from his examination and announced that here was nothing but a jumble of electronic instruments and devices, that would be my last moment. There would be a moment of blind rage, and I would cease to exist! Or, if my end did not come instantly, I could only expect a slower, more hideous vengeance for my deception. William George Thomas was not watching Doctor Von Steen; he was peering at me appraisingly, expectantly. I clenched my fists and braced myself against the denouement.

Von Steen put on his spectacles. He moved lamps closer. He stood for long minutes peering into the entrails of the aluminum case. His face was expressionless. Long slender fingers explored. He was deliberate. He turned away from the brain and peered at me.

"You," he said, "are an American electronic scientist?"

"Yes," said I.

"You have been associated with this—this production?"

"I have," said I.

"It was a rare privilege," he said, and his voice sounded sincere.

He returned to his peering and groping. The silence in the room was heavy. To me, the interval of waiting was unbearable; it was unbearable also to Toledo.

"What's the verdict? What's the verdict?" he demanded.

"Patience! Patience!" Von Steen said tartly.

He lifted out such portions as were movable, examining them one by one, nodding and muttering under his breath. He stood erect again as if to rest his back, and addressed me, not as an enemy, but as a fellow scientist.

"When your American brains learned to split the atom, to set up chain reaction, to wrest from nature one of its ultimate secrets, you did a surpassing thing. You accomplished what, I sometimes think, man was not meant to accomplish. Now you have done another thing; you have created a mechanical, an electronic intelligence. You have endowed base metals with the quality of reason. Or close to it. Herr Doktor, it may be you have ventured too far."

"You also," said I, "have striven to penetrate those secrets."

"And I am afraid," he said solemnly.

Von Steen returned to his scrutiny. The waiting for him to state his findings was torture. I had to fight myself to prevent myself from throwing up my arms and shouting, "Put an end to this! It's a fake! It's a fake!"

At last he sighed; he removed his spectacles; he turned to Balthasar Toledo. I stood tense. My waiting was at an end.

Doctor Von Steen smiled thinly at me.

"Mr. Toledo," he said, "I will stake my professional reputation—which is not inconsiderable—that this mechanism is authentic. It is the electronic brain."

I heard a gasp. It had issued from my own lips. It was incredible, beyond the bounds of possibility, but it had happened. This toy constructed to deceive had succeeded in its object. Doctor Von Steen pronounced it genuine.

My knees trembled and I pressed against the wall for support. It was a shock—an incredible shock. With my own ears I had heard this great scientist pronounce the bogus to be genuine. Either our electricians who had made the counterfeit brain were incredibly skillful or the scientific attainments of Moscow were puerile.

William George Thomas stirred in his chair so that it protested audibly. His little eyes had become big and round. It was at me that he stared, not at the incompetent scientist Von Steen. His blubber cheeks quivered like gelatin. He, it seemed, had suffered a shock equal to mine. In an instant he mastered himself; his face was bland. He even smiled faintly.

"That, Doctor Gimp," he said, "leaves us in the stratosphere without a guidance-control system. The watchword is now *sauve qui peut.*"

Sauve qui peut—the final command of despair. Everybody for himself. Save yourself if you can.

I recall, as if it were painted indelibly upon the retinas of my eyes, the appearance of that room and the exact position of all who were present. William George Thomas sat between the doors of the kitchen and the bedroom in which Melinna Brown was imprisoned. Doctor Von Steen stood at the table. Mr. Ken and Bubble Mouth stood shoulder to shoulder at the left of the fireplace. Otto occupied a position between table and outer door. The Mexican, Manuel, lounged in the kitchen door, and my back was against the westerly wall, facing Mr. Thomas. Balthasar Toledo confronted Von Steen, separated from him only by the width of the table.

"We have id," Otto said, suddenly exultant. "We have id.

Great credit rill come to me."

"They'll make you a commissar," sneered Toledo. He swung toward the fat man. "Now," he said, "we know where we're at. What's your proposition?"

"Do we know where we are?" Mr. Thomas countered. "Do we, indeed? First I would inquire how trustworthy is the opinion of Doctor Von Steen?"

"He would not have been sent," said Toledo, "if he were not competent."

"Oh, yes. Certainly." He perked his head to one side in an irritating manner. "Might I ask, Balthasar, how long and intimate has been your acquaintance with Doctor Von Steen? Old boyhood friends, perhaps?"

Toledo was impatient. "You know well that agents in the top brackets are not permitted to know each other."

"So I have been informed. Then the fact is you never have seen Doctor Von Steen before?"

"I do not need to have seen him before. He is Doctor Von Steen."

"Who," said the fat man slyly, "presented no credentials."

"There was no need," Von Steen said harshly. "The name is identification. The name is what you call the password."

Even I, not gifted in intrigue, could see the purpose of William George Thomas. It was to create a diversion—to gain time—to collect his forces, which had been shattered by Von Steen's pronouncement.

"There is a better means of identification," Mr. Thomas purred. "An identification by knowledge. A test to be passed as to qualification." He spread his fat fingers. "Now we have here a known scientist, a man accepted as eminent in electronics. None other than Doctor Gimp. I propose that he drop a plumb line into the depths of Doctor Von Steen's erudition. As for myself, I am not satisfied."

Mr. Ken interjected himself, smiling a sly Oriental smile.

"Mr. Thomas is a wise man. For myself, I think Mr. Thomas should be satisfied. I should like more cogent proof myself than a name, even a secret name. What says the great Ling Po?

'The mockingbird can sing the notes of a lark, but the plumage betrays the deception.' For myself I would like to see the plumage of Doctor Von Steen."

Balthasar Toledo hesitated. "We're wasting time," he said impatiently.

"To discover the truth is the noblest employment of time," said Mr. Ken.

"More Ling Po?" sneered Toledo.

"Precisely," said the Chinese. "Two or three little questions, Doctor Gimp. Difficult questions. It is but a reasonable precaution."

Toledo scowled at me. "Get on with it," he said shortly.

I racked my mind for questions that would test Doctor Von Steen's authenticity.

"What," I asked, "is a preset guidance system?"

Doctor Von Steen smiled. "It is a guidance-control system for a predetermined path wherein the path is set inside the missile before launching and cannot be adjusted after launching."

"What are its chief disadvantages?"

"Poor accuracy," he said promptly, "due to wind and instrument errors, including gyro drift."

"Describe," said I, "the so-called homing system."

"A homing system," he replied with a shrug, "is a guidance-control system wherein the direction of the missile can be changed after launching by a device in the missile which reacts to some distinguishing characteristic of the target. In the missile is a seeker which automatically keeps pointed at some property in the target such as light emissions, radio emissions, sound emissions, magnetic features and the like."

"Correct," said I. I propounded several other searching questions, which he answered in a satisfactory manner. Then I resorted to what I conceived to be the ultimate test. It was trickery. It was meaningless jargon. It was a question to which there was no correct answer save a derisive laugh.

"What," I asked, "is the coefficient of the isotope when subjected to the H-power of the Gamma ray when passing through the tropopause and entering the ionosphere if noctilucent clouds interpose an obstruction?"

It was sheer nonsense, meaningless, a jumble of words. The eyes of Doctor Von Steen bored into mine with a peculiar intentness. It was as if he willed that thought be transferred from his mind to mine. I glanced at his hands. They were clenched into fists and the knuckles were white.

"'Why, Doctor Gimp," he replied smoothly, as if the answer were elementary, "at that altitude the velocity of the cosmic ray nullifies the lateral, pressure of the G-layer and results in a maximum concentration of ions." He smiled at me thinly. "That, Doctor Gimp," he said, "should satisfy you of my knowledge and competence to a degree in which I might even be welcomed as a coworker in the laboratories of White Sands."

The man was an impostor. He had answered gibberish with gibberish. He was not Doctor Von Steen, Soviet scientist. But if not, who was he and what was his purpose? What had been his objective in pronouncing my counterfeit electronic brain genuine?

One point made itself evident to a mind accustomed to research and the use of reason: This man who represented himself to be Doctor Von Steen had come with the purpose of deceiving Balthasar Toledo and his accessories. His purpose must be inimical to them. It might not be friendly to me, but it was a thing of which a man of my intelligence must take advantage. I could lose nothing and might gain some advantage by refusing to unmask him. I nodded my head as if in understanding.

"Doctor Von Steen," said I, "has proved himself to be an electronic scientist of formidable attainments."

The man claiming the identity of Doctor Von Steen relaxed and shrugged.

"I am obligated to Doctor Gimp," he said.

"Satisfied?" Toledo asked of William George Thomas.

"Completely," the fat man replied. "Oh, fully and completely." He narrowed his eyes at me. "I, too," he said, "am not wholly unacquainted with the terminology of electronic science."

So Mr. Thomas also had detected the imposture and was

not exposing it! The man bewildered me. When he first came into the room, he had observed placidly that I was in a predicament. It was dawning upon me that he also found himself in a quandary.

"So," asked Toledo, "what is your proposition, William? And what puts you in a position to enforce your demands?"

"After profound consideration," the fat man said in his beautifully modulated voice, "I find I care to offer no dicker whatever. I do not like the climate. It oppresses me." He directed his glance toward me. "Gentlemen," he said agreeably, "I find that integrity, when wedded to a certain quantity of intelligence, is fatal to the sort of dickering I had in mind. I think I shall withdraw to a more salubrious milieu."

He put his hands on the arms of his chair and heaved himself to his feet. Manuel raised his drowsy head and shifted his position.

"Sit down!" commanded Balthasar Toledo.

"But," protested Mr. Thomas mildly, "I have no further interest here."

"We are interested in you!" Toledo snapped.

"As you say," the fat man replied in a tone of resignation.

"So you've no dicker to propose?" Toledo asked ironically. "What changed your mind, William?"

"Why," Thomas said, "this project seems to have reached a point of no return." He seated himself again. "I am a man of business. When I see no chance of profit I move promptly to cut my losses."

"Are we not," asked Mr. Ken, "losing time? Doctor Von Steen has given his opinion. He is ready to take delivery. . . . Are you not, Doctor?"

"I will take delivery at the border," said the German. "Escort me and this so-valuable object to the border."

"Where," Mr. Ken said suavely, "the money awaits?"

Doctor Von Steen closed the lid of the aluminum container. He reached for my suitcase and fitted the electronic brain in place.

"Ready," he said succinctly.

At that instant came an interruption. The door of the room in which Melinna was confined burst open and Melinna appeared. The Indian woman snatched at her to hold her back, but she eluded the brown hands.

"Why," she demanded angrily, "must I be shut up there with this woman? She sits and scowls! Why—"

She got no further. Bubble Mouth, who was closest to her, swung toward her, scowling, and struck her with the flat of his hand, so that she was thrown against the wall. Melinna uttered a little cry.

At the sight of this wanton mistreatment something seemed to detonate inside my head. The instinct of self-preservation, which had been strong within me, gave way to unreasoning rage. I quite forgot that these men were armed. I was careless of danger to myself. All prudence was swallowed up in such anger as I had known but once before. On the shelf of the fireplace stood an olla, a large earthenware jar. My hands lifted it, and with all my strength I hurled it at Bubble Mouth. My aim was good. It broke into a hundred pieces against the man's head. I must have been utterly reckless of consequences as I lurched toward Balthasar Toledo with clenched fists.

The scene was unnaturally distinct to me. I was aware of startled expressions, of men standing motionless in surprise. I seem to remember hand of William George Thomas appearing from the folds of his capacious garments with a small pistol in it. I heard the sound of its discharge and saw a tiny spot appear in the middle of the forehead of Mr. Ken.

As I continued my lunge toward Toledo, I heard the fat man's suave voice saying, as Mr. Ken slumped to the floor, "That is for grossly insulting a helpless guest."

It was the time lag again—that interval between perception and action. Before Toledo had his gun fully withdrawn, I held his wrist and struck with my other hand—struck with all my strength, reinforced by blind rage. At any instant I expected to suffer the impact of a bullet, but, somehow, I did not seem to care. Perhaps I had become a fatalist in that emergency. I would be killed anyhow, and my desire was to wreak as much damage upon my enemies as I could before I was stopped. Toledo fell, but as he did so he had his pistol fully unholstered, and fired from the floor. His aim was not good. Before he could fire again, a shot sounded from a quite impossible direction. Balthasar screamed in agony. His right hand, holding his weapon, seemed to disappear. The shot had been discharged by Manuel, the Mexican cook, not sleepy now, but erect and alert. Of the enemy, only the Slav, Otto, remained erect. But he cowered, terrified and harmless. Only Otto and the Communist scientist, Doctor Von Steen.

It was Von Steen who spoke to me. "That'll be plenty, doctor," he said. In his right hand he held a gun with which he seemed to threaten me. But he was not threatening me. Upon his bony face was a grim smile. "Quite a diversion you kicked up, Doctor Gimp," he said. "Premature, but effective."

I stood now, weak and shaking from reaction. I stared at Doctor Von Steen. I stared at the Mexican, Manuel, whose white teeth were gleaming. His was not the face of a shiftless peon, of a man to suffer without retaliation the kicks of an employer.

Recognition came. It was Senor Iturbe, brother of the Mexican policeman who had been murdered on the Golden State train.

I was bewildered.

"For a scientist," said Doctor Von Steen, "you pack quite a wallop." He shook his head in an admonitory manner. "You might have made a hash of it," he said. Then he smiled more pleasantly and extended his hand. "Maxwell French," he said, "of the FBI. Major Van Tuyl warned us you might be unpredictable."

The outer door burst open, and Major Van Tuyl lunged into the room. He was not alone. Suddenly the place seemed to be full of armed men. "What goes on?" Van Tuyl demanded. "I heard shots."

"Your Doctor Gimp," said the FBI agent, "lost his temper."

Van Tuyl eyed me dourly. "He does that," he said as though disgusted. "What a hunk of bait he turned out to be!" His thin lips twisted in a saturnine grin. "The doctor's got a grudge against me," he said to the FBI agent. "He thinks I left him in the soup."

"I hold no resentment," I said stiffly. "You could, however, have saved me hours of anxiety."

He shrugged. "The bleating of the kid," he said, "was needed to attract the tiger."

Relief such as I felt was an experience. To have rested for hours under the fear of death, and to have this fear suddenly and unexpectedly removed was a thing to move a man to weakness.

The breaking of tension left me depleted physically and bewildered mentally. I could not realize for a time that the emergency was past.

I saw men giving attention to Balthasar Toledo's shattered hand. I saw Otto in handcuffs. I looked with disbelief at the body of the unctuous Mr. Ken with a tiny, dark hole in his forehead. Bubble Mouth, consciousness recovered, was slumped against the wall with manacles upon his wrists. William George Thomas sat composedly in his chair.

"Gentlemen," he said, "with your permission, I will return to my bed in El Paso. It has been an exhausting, indeed a disappointing evening." He raised himself to his feet. "I have your permission to go?" he asked.

"Settle back in the harness," Major Van Tuyl said. "What makes you think you're in the clear?"

"Logic, sir—logic," said the fat man. "Can you lay your finger upon an action of mine which renders me liable to pains and punishments? Is there a scintilla of evidence which points to me as a wrongdoer? I fancy not."

Mr. French, the agent of the FBI, scowled at him. "We've long had our eyes on you, Thomas."

"But have they seen anything, Mr. French?"

"You're a slippery character."

"Anointed with oil," agreed Mr. Thomas. "May I point out that this evening I have been of some small service? I have paid a debt to Doctor Gimp, who once saved my life."

"We," said French, "could hold you for homicide."

"Now, Mr. French. Had I not shot the very dangerous Mr. Ken, he would have shot Doctor Gimp. His gun was in hand, ready to fire. Admitted that I am a devious character. I fish in troubled waters. I profit by the mistakes of others. I did not endeavor to steal your electronic brain. My purpose was to prey upon those who plotted to steal it. No, Mr. French, my character is without a stain."

French was disgruntled. "We've got nothing on you," he admitted. "But we can make this country too hot for you."

"I am removing myself from it," Mr. Thomas said. "There are other countries, more troubled than this, and less efficient in their vigilance. I have suffered grievous loss of cash and of time. I shall take my fishing equipment and my skill to another land, where trout are easier to take and game wardens are less vigilant." He advanced a step toward me. "I should like to shake your hand, Doctor Gimp. You have given me a new experience. You have been amusing, sir, but effective. It has been a pleasure to know you."

"I have profited from your acquaintance," I said to him, and took his hand. "Probably you are a bad man, Mr. Thomas, but somehow I like you."

"I shall remember your words with pleasure," he said. And then, "Good night, gentlemen. I have found you frustrating. I hope not to meet you again."

He waddled to the door, turned and waved a pudgy hand, and disappeared into the night.

"There," said Mr. French, "goes a man who could be of great service—if he had picked the right side. But he didn't. . . . I think we are finished here, Major Van Tuyl."

"A complete roundup," the major answered. He grinned at me. "The least we can do for you, Doctor Gimp, is to offer you—and Miss Brown—a ride to El Paso."

"We will be grateful," I assured him.

I looked across the room at Melinna. She was standing, quite composed. But there was a twinkle in her eyes.

"I left home in a hurry," she said to Major Van Tuyl. "I didn't bring a wrap. I wonder if someone could lend me a coat to keep me warm this chilly night?"

Van Tuyl's leathery face distorted itself into a saturnine grimace which was meant for a smile. "We can equip you with a coat," he said in a leering manner. "But I guess you won't need it. Doc Gimp'll volunteer to keep you warm."

"Doubtless," she said primly, "Doctor Gimp's enthalpy would be equal to the emergency, if he were equipped with an igniter."

"Enthalpy?" Van Tuyl said as if the word had been jarred out of him.

"Why, yes," said Melinna. "Enthalpy, major, is the sum of the internal and external energies of a substance or system, which is called the total heat."

Presently Melinna and I found ourselves snug in the back seat of a motorcar, moving briskly through the night toward the city of El Paso. After a time she spoke to me.

"Exhausted, doctor?" she asked in a tone which seemed to me to be odd.

"Quite," I answered.

"You act that way," she observed. "Are you too exhausted?"

"For what?" I asked.

"Well," she said, "as a preliminary, to snuggle. After what I've gone through, I could use a snuggle."

I placed my arm about her and drew her to me. She did not resist. On the contrary, she responded. Although, I suppose, a kiss is not included in a snuggle technically, I found her lips. Very pleasurable emotions engulfed me, and Melinna seemed equally moved. After an appreciable passage of time, she extricated herself from my arms and was breathless.

"Golly," she exclaimed, "you've got a swell set of enthalpy."

"Because," I responded ardently, "you are an effective igniter."

"Any further suggestion?" she asked. "Or are you just canoodling?" For once my mind was able to operate on the same plane as hers. It was encouraging to me. Definitely we were *en rapport.*

"My intentions—" said I, when she uttered an angry sound.

"If you say your intentions are honorable, I'll scream the roof down."

I was nonplused. "When," I demanded, "has an offer of marriage been obnoxious to a lady?"

"It's the way you do it," she said. "Give ear, my fatheaded darling, to words of wisdom. No marriage can be worth a hoot on honorable intentions. You can be as honorable as you like, but you've got to conceal it."

"What in heaven's name do you mean?"

"The basis," she said, "of a perfectly scrumptious married life is dishonorable intentions sanctified by wedding vows."

I cogitated upon that saying and found in it notable wisdom.

"When," I asked, "shall we subject ourselves to these essential vows?"

"Well," she said, "before the first of the month."

"Why that date?" I asked.

"Well," she said brazenly, "I've got us a house in White Sands. It'll be vacated on the first, and I put in for it. We really should be married before we move in."

"You've taken a house!" '

"Certainly," she answered. "I made up my mind some time ago we were going to need one. Me, my dear, I'm a forehanded woman."

I was speechless.

"One thing I insist on," she said peremptorily. "You've got to stay home nights and keep out of trouble. I can't be annoyed by your chasing spies and going all rash and adventurous on me. What I crave is serenity, science and—"

"Don't you say that other naughty word," I said. And then there followed another interlude of so-called snuggling.

"Do you remember," I asked Melinna, "the day you swung on the gate and ordered me to fight that boy?"

"Right well," she answered contentedly. "That's when I picked you. I knew you'd grow up to be a dandy fighter."

"But you've just admonished me to keep out of fights and

adventures."

"Right," she said promptly. "But what girl wants a man that can't deliver a sock if the need for it arises?"

"Er—mens sena in corpora sano," I said.

"Yes," she said, "but if you can manage it, I'd like a little more *corpora* and a trifle less *sano."*

"With you, my dear, as igniter, I fancy that can be managed," I said.

And then there was no more talk between us until we arrived at our destination.

Her final word to me as we parted was: "Good night, honey. See you at the altar."

And so, after some travail and not altogether unprofitable adventure, I returned to peaceful pursuits.

About the Author

CLARENCE BUDINGTON KELLAND, the legendary Golden Age author of mystery and romantic suspense, had enough careers for several men: attorney, reporter, manufacturer of clothespins, director of a major newspaper group, and more. Kelland became best known as a fiction writer, penning some 100 novels, and selling them as serials to the biggest and highest paying magazines of the time—like *The Saturday Evening Post, The American Magazine, Colliers,* and *Cosmopolitan.* Many were immortalized on film, of which the romantic suspense comedy and Oscar-winner, *Mr. Deeds Goes to Town,* is undoubtedly the most famous.

Kelland appeared alongside Agatha Christie, Rex Stout and Erle Stanley Gardner in the same magazines, but was the most popular of the four. *The New York Times* described Kelland's novels as "lively stories, designed to prick the jaded palate, that keep readers pleasantly entertained" and noted that "Kelland demonstrates the emotions of his lovers with a psychological penetration." *Kirkus Reviews* called his novels "Bright and breezy, with plus appeal for murder-mystery addicts." His magazine publishers kept besieging him for more novels because every time they serialized one of them (typically in 6-8 installments), circulation shot upward. Kelland obliged, and produced far more each year than his publisher (Harper and Row) could keep up with, leaving more than three dozen unpublished in book form when he died. His inimitable characters, trademark dialogue and deftly plotted stories, according to Harper, "made him an American tradition and won him more loyal, devoted readers than almost any other living author." Kelland, as ever self-depreciating, simply described himself as "the best second-rate writer in the world." His legions of fans, old and new, would likely disagree. There was nothing second-rate about his work.

Other
Clarence Budington Kelland Mystery Series
from
Digital Parchment Press

THE BIRTH OF TELEVISION MYSTERIES

Murder and the Key Man
Murder Makes and Entrance
Murder Makes a Mark

THE HISTORICAL MYSTERIES

The Cardiff Giant Affair
The Dangerous Angel Affair
The Monitor Affair

***THE WORKPLACE MYSTERIES* (Coming Soon)**

The Oil Field Mystery
The Showroom Mystery
The Newspaper Mystery
The Taxi War Mystery

FIRST BOOK EDITION
(Never before printed in book form! Coming Soon)

The Big Swindle
Face the Facts
The Murdered G-Man File
and
Mr. Deeds Goes to Town *(the book that inspired the Oscar-winning movie classic!)*

Printed in Great Britain
by Amazon